the Bagthorpe saga

the Bagthorpe saga

BOOK SEVEN

Bagthorpes Liberated

Helen Cresswell

Hodder Children's Books

a division of Hodder Headline plc

A Catalogue record for this book is
available from the British Library

ISBN 0340 71656 8

Typeset by Palimpsest Book Production Limited,
Polmont, Stirlingshire

Printed and bound in Great Britain by
Clays St Ives, plc

Hodder Children's Books
A Division of Hodder Headline plc
338 Euston Road
London NW1 3BH

For Michael Thomas

1

When the Bagthorpes arrived home from their abortive holiday in Wales it was dark, and nearly everyone was in a bad temper. This was mainly because of the travel arrangements.

The minibus that took the Bagthorpes and their excess baggage down to Wales had been booked for the return journey in six weeks' time. They were now decamping after as many days. Mrs Bagthorpe had accordingly rung and cancelled the minibus. This was for two reasons. One was that nobody wished to risk getting the same driver who had been full of pithy comment about their Matterhorn of luggage. This had taken a full two hours to stow and was like, he said, trying to get a bleeding gallon into a pint pot.

Since then, of course, Mr Bagthorpe had acquired a further mountain of expensive junk, including such items as stags' heads and stuffed birds in glass cases.

'On this occasion,' he pointed out, 'it would be like trying to get the bleeding Atlantic into a pint pot.'

Mrs Bagthorpe had booked a self-drive van, 'Which you, Henry, will have to drive,' she told him.

'What about us?' demanded Rosie. 'Where're we going to sit?'

The answer to this question, so far as she, Tess and Jack were concerned, was in among the junk at the back of the van. (There was in fact a spare seat next to Mr Bagthorpe, but nobody wished to occupy it.) The rest were squashed into the family estate car, driven by Mrs Bagthorpe. Frequent stops were made on account of Grandma's weak bladder.

As the sun set, and the countryside around became familiar, Mrs Bagthorpe found herself able to Think Positively with hardly any effort at all.

'Oh, lovely, we're nearly home!' she told her passengers.

'After a really lovely holiday,' said William bitterly.

'*I* have enjoyed the holiday, William,' Grandma said. This was probably true. Armageddon had followed on Armageddon fast enough to satisfy even her. 'I feel thoroughly refreshed.'

'Well, *I* don't,' said Mrs Fosdyke. 'Begging your pardon. '*Ome*'ll seem like a holiday, after that. Is Mr Bagthorpe going to see me 'ome?'

'Er – when?' inquired her perplexed employer. 'In what way?'

'I ain't setting foot in that 'ouse,' said Mrs Fosdyke, 'till it's been gone through thorough. *Anyone* could be in there.'

'Er – such as who, Mrs Fosdyke dear?'

'Rapers,' replied Mrs Fosdyke flatly. 'And murderers. What about that man escaped that'd 'atcheted five women?'

'But that was weeks ago!' protested Mrs Bagthorpe.

''E's somewhere lurking,' said Mrs Fosdyke darkly.

'Certainly he is,' put in Grandma. 'We have ourselves been burgled remember, Laura, and that when the house was occupied. Henry must certainly search Mrs Fosdyke's house most thoroughly before she enters. We would none of us wish to lose her – and particularly in so unpleasant a way.'

This was not strictly true. Several members of the family would have welcomed the loss of Mrs Fosdyke, in however gruesome a manner. Mr Bagthorpe, however, had no choice but to comply with Mrs Fosdyke's demand.

Both vehicles drew up outside Mrs Fosdyke's house. A ripple of drawn aside curtains ran down the road. The occupants of the van, who had been warned of this minor hold-up, got out to stretch their legs. Mrs Fosdyke was already standing on the pavement clutching her handbag, a forlorn figure under the street lamp. Mr Bagthorpe, cursing under his breath, himself got out.

'Come on, then!' he told her ungraciously. 'Got your key?'

Mrs Fosdyke shook her head. Mr Bagthorpe stared.

'Well, get looking for it, quick!' he told her. 'Get rummaging in your bag!'

She shook her head again.

'It ain't in there. I 'id it.'

'*Id* it? *Hid* it? What d'you mean?'

'In the garden. I've forgot where.'

'You've – what?'

'Anyone can forget things,' said Mrs Fosdyke defensively. 'What I've been through these past days, wonder is I ain't forgot my own name!'

By now the whole Bagthorpe contingent was crowded on the pavement and windows were opening along Coldharbour Road. The neighbours could see what was going on, all right, but now wished to hear, as well.

'Now try to think, Mrs Fosdyke,' urged Mrs Bagthorpe Positively. 'Under a stone, perhaps, by the back door?'

'Never!' stated Mrs Fosdyke flatly. 'I ain't that daft. *All* murderers look under stones by the back door.'

'What about under that garden gnome we got you last Christmas?' suggested Jack.

Again she shook her head.

'Hell fire!' exclaimed Mr Bagthorpe. 'Have we now to play Hunt the Thimble in your back garden in the pitch dark?'

'Get the torches!' said William.

'Oh dear!' said his mother. 'Would you like to come and spend the night with us, Mrs Fosdyke dear? Then we can search at leisure in the daytime. It would be rather fun – I could offer a small prize to the finder.'

'Good thinking, Laura!' said her husband, who

under normal circumstances would himself threaten to leave home at such a suggestion.

But Mrs Fosdyke was shaking her head.

'I want to go 'ome,' she said. 'I want to spend the night with me feet under me own table.'

Jack, conjuring up a picture of this, let out a snort. His mother gave him a sharp look.

'Find the torches, Jack!' she ordered.

This was no easy matter, given the quantity of luggage. Rosie, Tess and William all helped, and there was a great deal of yelling and rolling of stags' heads into the road. The neighbours were enchanted. They had abandoned their television sets for the real life drama being played out in Coldharbour Road.

'You did not, I suppose, consider putting the key into your handbag, like any normal person?' asked Mr Bagthorpe bitterly.

Mrs Fosdyke ignored him.

'And my suitcase!' she shrieked to the unloaders.

Mr Bagthorpe, cursing inaudibly, turned on his heel and was soon rampaging in Mrs Fosdyke's front garden, furiously shaking trees and shrubs.

'I ain't 'id it in a tree!' she screamed, as a hail of leaves and twigs flew about her.

'Then where have you 'id it, woman!' he bellowed. 'I'm going to break a window! Where's a brick?'

He lurched towards the house, and Mrs Fosdyke screeched, 'No! No! Don't let 'im!'

'Stop, Henry!' commanded Mrs Bagthorpe in ringing tones. 'Stop, I say!'

'There is one thing certain,' observed Grandma, who was enjoying the pantomime hugely, 'any murderer concealed in that house has had ample warning of his discovery.'

'That's true,' agreed Mrs Bagthorpe. 'He may have already escaped through the back door.'

'The door is *locked*, Laura,' Grandma reminded her. 'He is by now no doubt selecting the largest kitchen knife he can discover.'

'Here's two torches,' Jack said. 'But their batteries seem to be flat.'

This, given the number of nocturnal hours spent ghost hunting at Ty Cilion Duon, was hardly surprising.

'Oh! Oh dear! Then we must search by the light of the moon,' said Mrs Bagthorpe weakly.

'There *is* no moon, Laura,' her husband told her. 'And I for one do not intend to crawl on my hands and knees all night in the pitch dark among earthworms and garden gnomes. Where's a brick – I shall smash a window!'

He cast wildly about him for an odd brick. The shock must have jolted Mrs Fosdyke's memory, because she screeched, 'No! I've remembered! I know where I put it!'

A silence fell over the Bagthorpes and the attentive neighbours as they awaited her revelation.

'It come to me in a flash,' said Mrs Fosdyke smugly. 'I was ever so cunning. First I thought, "Under a stone by the back door." And then I thought, "No, that's where all robbers and murderers look." Then I thought under the gnome, and then I thought, "No, 'cos I ain't ever put it there before, and I might forget!"'

She looked hopefully about her audience for applause of her wisdom and foresight. Mr Bagthorpe leant wearily against the wall of the house and banged his head softly on it.

'Might forget! Ye gods! Might forget, she says!'

'Well,' continued Mrs Fosdyke, 'what I thought then was "Where is the last place in this garden a raper or a murderer would look for a key?" And you know what I came up with?'

Again she looked expectantly about her.

'Go on, tell us, Mrs F.,' urged William.

'I put it,' said Mrs Fosdyke, 'under the fourth lobelia from the left!'

The triumph in her voice seemed to indicate her certain knowledge that while a felon might be moved to search under the second lobelia from the left, say, or the fifth from the right, he would never, till the sea ran dry or it rained mint sauce, consider any lobelia fourth from the left.

'Eureka!' said Mr Bagthorpe bitterly.

'At least, I *think* it was fourth from the left . . .' went on Mrs Fosdyke, a note of doubt creeping in. 'I'm just about sure it was.'

'Go and fetch it, Jack dear,' said his mother swiftly. 'And you, Henry, take Mrs Fosdyke's suitcase.'

'Why?' he demanded.

'Because it is heavy,' she replied, 'and you are a gentleman. At any rate – a man.'

Mr Bagthorpe, muttering about blatant sexism and discrimination, sullenly picked up the case and started to drag it towards the house.

'We will wait for you, Henry,' Grandma told him. 'After all, you will be required to search our own premises before we enter.'

Jack and William, who did not for a single moment believe that Unicorn House was being stalked by a mass murderer, volunteered to do this. Grandma instantly vetoed the suggestion.

'The kind of fiend who will kill five innocent women will certainly have no qualms about slaughtering two innocent boys,' she said.

This set up a complicated argument both about the predilections of mass murderers, and the claimed innocence of Jack and William.

'I bet they weren't innocent even when they were babies!' Rosie said. 'Why can't Zero go in and sniff the murderer out? And why is it always *us* that get ghosts and flocks of sheep in the house, and murderers?'

'Because the Bagthorpe Family is a great Tragic House, dear,' Grandma told her. 'It has ever been so. It attracts calamity as a flag pole attracts lightning.'

'You mean like Oedipus, and that lot?' asked Jack. 'At least no one's had their eyes put out yet.'

'Not yet, Jack dear,' replied Grandma, faintly wistful.

Mr Bagthorpe was in Mrs Fosdyke's house a long time. He was in there so long that speculation began as to whether, in fact, there was a mass murderer in there who had by now notched up a further two victims to his score.

'That would make seven,' said Rosie. 'Would that be a record?'

The Bagthorpes as a clan were very keen on records, though no one had so far dreamed of being involved in one so lurid.

At this moment there came the all too familiar sound of a police siren. The Bagthorpes and bemused inhabitants of Cold-harbour Road turned to see the car, blue light flashing, turn into the road and advance rapidly towards them. It screeched to a halt behind the hired van, and two officers leapt out.

'Ah, thank heaven! Law and Order at last!' exclaimed Grandma delightedly, her cup running over. 'This way, officers, this way!'

'Now then,' said Officer One. 'What's going on?'

Mrs Bagthorpe stepped swiftly forward.

'Good evening, Officer,' she greeted him. 'May I introduce myself? I am Mrs Laura Bagthorpe – perhaps you recognize me? I am a magistrate on the Aysham Bench?'

The officer regarded her keenly, as if memorizing her features for an Identikit picture.

'No, madam, I can't say I do,' said Officer One. 'Are you here in your – er – official capacity?'

'Oh no!' cried Mrs Bagthorpe merrily. 'These

are my family – we are just returning from holiday.'

'This your house, then?' Officer Two indicated
Mrs Fosdyke's residence, where an upstairs light had
just been switched on.

'Oh no – no! We were just seeing Mrs Fosdyke
home, and my husband is checking the house for
possible murderers or rapers – I mean rapists.'

The officers brightened at this intelligence.

'Very unwise,' said One. 'You should have called
us immediately.'

'We'd better radio back to base,' said Two, and
made back to the car. In his haste he failed to see a
stag's head, tripped and fell heavily to the ground. His
colleague hurried to his assistance and helped him to
his feet. The pair stood looking incredulously down
at the cause of his fall. Two bent and picked it up.

'It's a cow's head!'

'Stag's,' corrected One. 'This yours?'

'It's father's,' piped up Rosie. 'He bought it by
mistake. You can have it if you like.'

Ignoring this generous offer the police moved to
the rear of the van and peered in through the open
doors. They themselves had very powerful torches,
and their beams played into the shadowy interior,
eerily picking out its contents.

The Bagthorpes, standing at a little distance, could
hear snatches of their exchange.

'Rum lot of stuff to bring back off holiday . . .'

'There's another of them dead heads . . .'

'Could be a haul of antiques . . .'

'You don't hire a van this size, just to go on holiday . . .'

They moved away from the van and began to inspect the estate car, still playing their torches.

'Look!'

'A body!'

The relentless beams lit the peacefully sleeping features of Grandpa, who had slept for most of the journey and failed to be awoken by the recent racket.

The officers straightened and turned to the waiting Bagthorpes.

'This your vehicle, madam?'

'Yes, officer, and that is—'

'There's someone in there.'

'My husband, Inspector,' Grandma told him.

'And what you mean is that whoever murdered him is – in there?'

He indicated Mrs Fosdyke's house, and as he did so Mr Bagthorpe appeared from the rear. Both officers stiffened.

'Stand back!' they ordered, and rapidly did so themselves.

'My son, my son, thank heaven he is safe!' exclaimed Grandma, for the benefit of the police and spectators. She overplayed the scene by hastening forward and attempting to embrace Mr Bagthorpe as he came through the gate.

'Hell's bells, Mother, what's the game?' he demanded.

He struggled furiously to free himself, and in doing so caught sight of the police over her left shoulder.

What then followed very nearly ended in his arrest. Mr Bagthorpe had never learned that when dealing with the police it is wise to be courteous and even, on occasion, obsequious. Nobody could truthfully deny that the Bagthorpes had been creating a disturbance in Coldharbour Road, and that the neighbour who had called the police (having heard words like 'robber' and 'murderer' freely bandied about) had acted quite correctly. When in the wrong, instead of smoothing things over, Mr Bagthorpe acted like a cornered animal and started snarling. This he now proceeded to do.

He strode about, completely ignoring the police's efforts to question him, picking up stray stags' heads and onion strings and hurling them into the back of the van. He saw the crowd of onlookers and pitched into them to such effect that they cowered away, and some ran back into their houses and locked themselves in.

The police insisted on rousing Grandpa, to satisfy themselves that he was not a body. When they did so Mr Bagthorpe (who cared not a fig whether his father slept or woke) ran at them, and would have pummelled them with his fists had not his wife restrained him. Grandpa, gently woken by Two, opened his eyes and beamed with seraphic sweetness.

'There!' yelled Mr Bagthorpe. 'Now look what you've done!'

Grandpa looked vaguely about him, smiled again, and went back to sleep.

It was perhaps fortunate that at this juncture Mrs Fosdyke reappeared, still wearing her hat.

'This way, this way!' she screeched, beckoning furiously.

The bewildered police, still half-expecting a body to be found, obeyed.

It later emerged that Mr Bagthorpe, while searching the premises for a mass murderer, had half-heartedly sauntered about the house, peering into the oven and the deep freeze, and so on, but had flatly refused to look either in Mrs Fosdyke's wardrobe or under her bed. These, she claimed, were the prime areas of risk. Clearly Mr Bagthorpe had secretly thought so himself, and having no real wish to encounter a homicidal maniac had studiously avoided them, leaving the aforesaid maniac to emerge later and (hopefully) murder Mrs Fosdyke.

While the police were conducted to her house the Bagthorpes made their getaway. They piled into their vehicles and shot out of Coldharbour Road like bats out of hell.

As they turned in through the gates of Unicorn House and went up the familiar drive each one of them, though they would never (with the exception of Mrs Bagthorpe) have admitted it, felt a sense of relief, of homecoming. Unicorn House was by no means a haven of rest, but it had never, so far, housed ghosts or flocks of sheep. They all, except Grandpa, clambered out and gazed fondly up at its darkened windows. Zero ran madly hither and thither, sniffing rapturously.

'My radio mast's still there,' said William. 'It's to be hoped Anonymous from Grimsby is.'

'The key, Henry dear,' said Mrs Bagthorpe. 'Oh, isn't it lovely to be home! I feel as if I had been away for a million years!'

There were certainly enough (full) milk bottles ranged down the drive to give this impression. Some-one had evidently forgotten to cancel the milk.

The milkman was no lover of the Bagthorpes. He was regularly yelled at by Mr Bagthorpe for rattling his crates, had been chased by Billy Goat Gruff and bitten several times by Grandma's cat. Nor did he care for Mrs Fosdyke. She constantly accused him of leaving the wrong number of bottles, and when she paid him always counted the change twice, out loud, in a manner he found insulting. When, therefore, the family had gone away without cancelling their order, he gleefully realized that they had played right into his hands. If he left the usual six pints a day for six weeks, the whole length of the drive of Unicorn House could well be lined with bottles on their return.

If they complained, he had his answer ready. He would reply that he was not a mind reader, nor was he paid to be, and that whether customers took their milk in or left it outside was no concern of his. The customer, he would say, is always right. That the Bagthorpes should have to pay for two hundred and fifty pints of curdled milk struck him as no more than their just deserts. He hoped they had forgotten to cancel their newspapers and comics, too. (They had.)

Mrs Bagthorpe looked dubiously at the regiment of bottles, but thought it wise not to draw them to the attention of her husband, who appeared not to have noticed them.

'The key, dear,' she said again.

'What d'you mean, key?' said Mr Bagthorpe irritably. 'You've got it.'

'No, dear. You were the last out. You went back for your ionizer, remember?'

Mr Bagthorpe had installed an ionizer in his study to suck up Mrs Fosdyke's hostile vibrations which if allowed to accumulate would, he claimed, block his creativity.

'Oh, come *on*!' begged Rosie. 'Hurry up! You can't have lost the key!'

'Perhaps you hid it under the fourth lobelia from the left, Father?' suggested William.

'That would mean the formation of a cluster,' said Tess obscurely. 'A meaningful coincidence. There may be other keys lost.'

'Shut up!' Mr Bagthorpe told her rudely. 'Hand over the key, Laura, and let's get in.'

'There is some urgency, Henry,' said Grandma. 'My bladder, remember.'

'Oh, hang your bladder!' he snapped. 'There are plenty of bushes.'

'Among which,' she told him, 'could be lurking a murderer, or a rapist.'

'Don't *you* start,' he told her. 'And even if there were, it'd be for *him* to look out, not you. Ha!'

'You could take Zero with you, Grandma,' Jack offered.

'I am fast losing all patience,' said Mrs Bagthorpe. 'Henry, turn out your pockets and find that key.'

'To do so would be to search for a non-existent needle in a haystack,' he returned. 'Turn out *your* pockets, and that carpet bag you carry round with you!'

'If I did not have to safeguard my personal correspondence from your poking and prying I would not have to carry it about with me,' she said. 'I could have a normal-sized handbag, like any other woman.'

A Row was brewing. Jack, who was hopeless at joining in Rows properly, wandered away. He could not explain what impulse made him do so, but he went right up to the front door and turned the handle. He pushed, and the door opened – though not easily, on account of the piled-up post, newspapers and periodicals behind it.

Only Rosie saw this.

'Oh Jack!' she screamed. 'You're brilliant! Look, everyone – the door's open!'

The hubbub died as the Bagthorpes turned and saw the open door. They stared.

'There you are!' said Mr Bagthorpe to his wife.

'That mutton-headed son of yours had the key all along!'

'I didn't!' Jack protested. 'All I did was turn the knob and push!'

The silence now became absolute, except for Zero's noisy snuffing. All present slowly took in the implications of the thing. There were only two possible. Either Unicorn House had been broken into during their absence, or the Bagthorpes had gone to Wales for six weeks leaving their front door unlocked.

2

None of the Bagthorpes had been interested in the possibility of Mrs Fosdyke's house sheltering a mass murderer, but this was an altogether different matter.

'You had better go in there, Henry, and make a thorough search,' said Grandma. 'It would be prudent to arm yourself first.'

'I'll go with you, Father,' said Jack bravely.

'But there are *millions* of places for a murderer to hide!' Rosie wailed. 'Our house is miles bigger than Fozzy's! He could even be up the chimney!'

'Certainly he could,' Grandma nodded. 'Jack, let Thomas out of his basket, please. By now his bladder must be in the same state as my own.'

'Hell's bells, Mother,' said Mr Bagthorpe, 'will you stop burbling on about your bladder!'

'As a thorough search of the house will take half the night,' went on Grandma, ignoring him, 'I think that you, Laura, should drive me back to Mrs Fosdyke's. I can take shelter with her, and use her conveniences.'

'I think we should all stay here, at least until Henry has turned on the electricity,' said Mrs Bagthorpe. 'Once we have lighting, things will seem very different.'

'*You* go in and switch the lights on,' Mr Bagthorpe told her. 'Why me?'

'Because you, Henry, are a man.'

'It does not require the strength of Atlas to press down a couple of switches,' he returned. 'A child could do it.'

'Why don't we all go in?' suggested his wife. 'There is strength in numbers. We can all arm ourselves with tennis rackets and fishing rods, and so on. It would be a kind of game.'

'Good thinking, Mother!' William went to the back of the van and began to pull out items that might serve as weapons and hand them round.

'But we haven't got any knives and guns!' cried Rosie, shrinking back from a proffered racket that had been severely mangled by Billy Goat Gruff.

'You and I will stay out here, dear,' Grandma told her. 'As the oldest and the youngest. How I wish darling Daisy were here! She would walk into that house without a qualm. She has no fear of any living thing.'

'I agree, Mother,' said Mr Bagthorpe. 'The most hardened criminal on earth would have to look to himself when she's around. Ha!'

'Come on,' said William impatiently. 'Let's get it over with!'

The Bagthorpes, armed with their assorted weaponry, cautiously advanced to the half-open door. They were lit from behind by headlights, but the interior before them was in total darkness. They stopped and listened.

'Where are the switches?' whispered Tess.

'In the cupboard under the stairs,' her mother whispered back.

This was not, of course, good news. Cupboards under stairs are notorious places of concealment for anything from murderers to skeletons.

Inch by inch William pushed the door wider, and one by one the rest followed. They tiptoed over the polished boards, wincing at every creak. There was a muffled curse as Mr Bagthorpe tripped over Zero. They were all poised to turn and run.

Jack, putting out his hands as if playing Blind Man's Buff, encountered warm flesh, and let out a yelp.

'Ssssshhhh!' came a concerted hiss.

Progress was slow. Everyone was trying to let everyone else go first. By the time they reached the far end of the hall Jack felt rather as Hannibal might, having crossed the Alps.

'I think we're there,' whispered Mrs Bagthorpe. 'Open the door, Henry.'

He hesitated. He did not usually feel that discretion is the better part of valour, but was inclined to now. He actually knocked on the door.

Silence.

'Is anybody there?' He sounded as if he were trying to raise a spirit.

If there were, he wasn't answering.

Without warning Mr Bagthorpe seized the handle and threw the door open, thereby knocking over Tess and Jack like skittles.

'Quick!' yelled Mr Bagthorpe. 'I've thrown the switches!'

He clearly believed this to be tantamount to having pulled the pin of a hand grenade.

'The light! Find the light switch!'

It was William who succeeded in doing this. Light flooded the hall, revealing Jack and Tess still on their hands and knees, and Mr Bagthorpe bent almost double, with his arms wrapped over his head for protection. His wife had her eyes closed and was either praying, Breathing, or both. Zero was running round in circles with his nose to the ground, as if tracking a recent game of ring o' roses.

'Is it all clear?' asked Mr Bagthorpe. Nobody bothered to reply. He straightened up and unwrapped his arms from his head, feeling rather silly.

'There!' he said triumphantly. 'That's done it!'

'On the contrary, Henry, it has only just begun,' contradicted Grandma, who had advanced as far as the front door. If any of her family were slaughtered, she could then act as police witness. 'The whole house must now be combed, from cellars to attics. Kindly search the downstairs cloakroom first, William dear. What a sore trial it is to have a weak bladder!'

'Amen to that,' said her son. 'We're all stuck with it. All right, search that. Then my study. Then the kitchen.'

A Plan of Campaign was already taking shape in his mind.

William kicked open the door of the lavatory, and it could be seen at a glance that no murderer was in there.

'You do my study, Jack,' Mr Bagthorpe ordered. 'Fast.'

Jack obeyed. A cautious scan of the room from the doorway revealed nothing untoward. The study was in the customary disorder that was the despair of Mrs Bagthorpe and Mrs Fosdyke, but beloved by its occupant.

'Shakespeare never used filing systems,' he would say. 'Nor the soaring eagle in his flight. To file is the mark of a fool.'

When he lost or mislaid things, as he frequently did, he would blame Mrs Fosdyke.

Grandma now emerged.

'I am ready to be taken to Mrs Fosdyke's, Laura,' she announced. 'I cannot remain here and be put at risk.'

'Can I come too?' Rosie begged.

William, Tess and Jack all considered searching for a mass murderer preferable to another dose of Mrs Fosdyke, and opted to stay on. Rosie was made to recapture Little Tommy and put him back in his basket, because Grandma said that the kind of man who hatcheted five people would stop at nothing, even dispatching an innocent cat.

When Mrs Bagthorpe's contingent arrived back at Mrs Fosdyke's the police had left, to Grandma's secret disappointment. One of her motives in returning had been the hope of making a statement.

'That is strange . . .' murmured Mrs Bagthorpe. 'There seem to be no lights on.'

'P'raps they've arrested Fozzy and taken her to prison,' ventured Rosie hopefully.

'Or perhaps both police officers and Mrs Fosdyke have been murdered,' suggested Grandma, equally hopefully.

'Then where is their vehicle?' asked Mrs Bagthorpe.

'Used as a getaway car,' Grandma told her. 'The perfect cover.'

The trio trooped round to the back, which was also in darkness. Rosie knocked at the door.

'Surely she cannot already be in bed and asleep?' said Mrs Bagthorpe.

'She's hardly had time to take her hat off,' said Rosie. She had a sudden vision of Mrs Fosdyke spending the night with her legs under her own table and her hat on, and giggled.

'It is not funny, Rosie,' Mrs Bagthorpe told her. She always tried to Think Positively, but was now finding this difficult. Suppose something *had* happened to Mrs Fosdyke? Who, then, would clean the house, wash and iron, polish the brass and silver, cook the meals? The answer to these questions was stark and uncompromising. She, Mrs Bagthorpe, would have to do all these things. What then of her work as Stella Bright, with an Agony Column, and as JP on the Aysham Bench?

'Where can she be?' she cried desperately. 'Knock again, Rosie! No – look under the fourth lobelia to the left!'

'What a perfectly dotty suggestion, Laura,' said Grandma. 'Mrs Fosdyke is scarcely likely to have departed on another holiday already.'

'Oh, she must be in there!' cried Mrs Bagthorpe. She hurried off to the front of the house, and stood staring up at what she knew to be Mrs Fosdyke's bedroom window. No light showed behind the drawn curtains. Mrs Bagthorpe remembered her husband's earlier threats about bricks.

'I shall throw a pebble up at her window!' she exclaimed. 'Yes – that is the answer!'

She stooped and began scrabbling about in Mrs Fosdyke's small rockery.

Mrs Bagthorpe had read of people being roused by pebbles thrown at their windows, but had never herself done this. She must have had a very hazy idea of what constituted a pebble, because the stone she selected, though one of the smaller ones, was more like half a brick.

She stepped back on to the tiny patch of grass, stared desperately at the blank window, and threw the 'pebble' with all her might.

There was an almighty crack, followed by the splintering of glass. A few fragments tinkled on to the path, the rest went into Mrs Fosdyke's bedroom. Mrs Bagthorpe's hand flew to her mouth.

'Mother!' screamed Rosie.

'Laura!' breathed Grandma in tones of unholy glee.

The inhabitants of Coldharbour Road, already jumpy, were at their doors and windows in a flash.

'It's a break in!'

'Look — there they are!'

'Call the police!'

'Oh no! No! No!' Mrs Bagthorpe ran out of the garden into the road. She stood directly under the street lamp and tilted back her face to identify herself.

'It is I, Laura Bagthorpe! You all know me!'

They did indeed — by repute. Unfortunately, the reputation of all the Bagthorpes rested on the say so of Mrs Fosdyke. Over the years she had related bloodcurdling accounts of their long saga of fires, floods, burglaries, goats making puddles. The residents of Coldharbour Road were not comforted.

'Look at that window — smashed to smithereens!'

'Must've chucked a whole brick!'

'Is Glad in there, d'you think?'

'Mrs Fosdyke is alive and well!' cried Mrs Bagthorpe in ringing tones.

'Where is she, then?'

'Glad! Glad!'

Concern for Mrs Fosdyke ran high. This was surprising. The things Mrs Fosdyke had told the Bagthorpes about her neighbours had never been flattering. She was, she said, 'picked on' by them. She did not know why. She thought it might be jealousy.

'Thought you lot was supposed to be in Wales.'

'Thought Glad'd gone for six weeks!'

'Oh dear, oh dear!' Mrs Bagthorpe glanced swiftly back at the house. If Mrs Fosdyke were in there, and alive, she would surely by now be up and out and putting in her own twopenn'orth.

Mrs Bagthorpe turned again to face her hostile audience.

'I strongly urge everyone not to call the police,' she said. 'Nothing at all has happened, except a slight accident with a window. There is an offence known as wasting police time.'

She was full into her magisterial stride.

'I advise you all to return to your homes. We shall now do so ourselves.'

With these words she marched purposefully to the car and got in. Rosie scrambled into the back seat beside the still peacefully slumbering Grandpa.

'He must be Selectively Deaf even in his sleep,' she thought.

Grandma's progress to the car was slower. She was reluctant to abandon what had seemed a very promising scenario. By lingering she hoped to give the police time to arrive, if they had already been called.

She eventually got into the car and sank back in her seat, disappointed. Mrs Bagthorpe immediately started up and drove off.

'There is one thing, Laura,' Grandma remarked as they turned out of the road without a flashing blue light in sight, 'your fellow members on the

Bench are going to be interested to hear of this episode.'

'If old Fozzy was in there, you could've killed her!' Rosie contributed.

'Precisely,' nodded Grandma. 'Mrs Fosdyke deserved better, Laura.'

Mrs Bagthorpe, lips tightly compressed, drove on. As she was going through the village she thought she caught a glimpse of a red sports car being driven furiously in the opposite direction. Only Uncle Parker would drive at that speed through a built-up area. But the Parkers, she knew, were still comfortably ensconced in their five star castle in Wales. She dismissed it as hallucination, brought on by shock.

When the party drew up for the second time that night in front of Unicorn House, several ground-floor windows were now ablaze with lights. Mrs Bagthorpe drew a deep breath and said Positively, 'Ah – that looks more like home!'

'The foulest deeds may befall under the brightest light,' said Grandma darkly. She managed to make it sound like a quotation, possibly from Shakespeare. In fact, she had just made it up.

'Bring in Little Tommy,' she ordered. 'The night is growing chill.'

They all disembarked, leaving Grandpa still fast asleep in the growing chill. They were greeted in the hall by Tess.

'You're back soon,' she told them. 'Mother, make Father come out and help.'

Jack and William emerged from the sitting room which they had just searched, even looking inside the grand piano, in case the intruder should be a dwarf.

'He's in there!' Tess pointed to the study door. 'And he ought to be the first to go upstairs. He's a man!'

It emerged that once his study and the kitchen had been declared danger free zones, Mr Bagthorpe had set about making a large flask of coffee. Clutching this, a packet of digestives and a bottle of Scotch, he had gone back to his study and locked himself in.

'I am in the grip of inspiration!' he had declared. 'Keep the noise down, for pity's sake. And let me know when it's safe to go to bed.'

On receiving this intelligence his wife, her nerves already severely strained, became unhinged. She rushed to the study door, rattled the handle in vain, then beat on the door with her fists.

'Henry! Henry! Come out this minute!'

'Go away!' came Mr Bagthorpe's reply. 'Am I to have no peace?'

'There is the whole house to be searched from top to bottom!' she shrieked.

'You do it!' came the reply.

'And – and Mrs Fosdyke has vanished!'

'Hallelujah! Amen!'

'Why don't we go round the back and shove a brick through his window?' suggested William.

'You do that,' came his father's voice, 'and I shall personally dismember you.' Pause. 'And your benighted mast!'

'Jack, dear, are you sure the sitting room is quite safe?' asked Grandma. 'If so, I shall go and stretch out on the sofa. One of you might perhaps make me some tea. It is a pity Henry is such a coward. He is yellow to the core.'

'Yellow yourself!' shouted Mr Bagthorpe. 'Yellow the lot of you! And shut up, will you! I'm trying to think!'

'I don't believe you!' cried his wife passionately. 'You are yellow and idle – and oh, how shall I survive without Mrs Fosdyke?'

She began to weep.

'You go and sit down, Mother,' Jack told her. 'Look – I know what we'll do. We'll go upstairs in a sort of chain, and one of us stop here by the phone. Then, if the first person in the chain sees or hears anything, we can pass the message back, and the one by the phone dials 999.'

'Bags I the phone,' said his siblings simultaneously.

'I think Rosie ought to be by the phone,' Jack said. 'I'll go first, with Zero.'

'Oh, you are brave!' exclaimed Rosie admiringly.

Jack was inclined to agree with her. At the outset he had not believed that there was a mass murderer or robber in anybody's house. Now, he was not so sure. The front door, after all, had been left unlocked for nearly a week. There could be several people up there.

He switched on the light at the bottom of the stairs, and could at least now see that his way to the first turn was clear.

'Come on, William, you keep about five steps behind me. Tess, you start up when we reach the first landing.'

'Kindly search my room first,' Grandma called after them. 'I, after all, have most to lose.'

Jack began stamping up the stairs. He made as much noise as possible, to give any intruder ample time to escape down a convenient drainpipe. He also kept saying loudly, 'Come on, Zero! Good boy! Find, Zero!'

It was at times like this that he wished Zero had a more impressive sounding name. Something that made him sound more like an Alsatian, or bull mastiff. Jaws, perhaps, or Killer.

When he reached the first landing he switched on another light.

'Come on!' he said loudly.

William was at least eight steps behind him, and Tess had not even started up. When he reached the first floor he looked warily to left and right. Following instructions, he stamped first towards Grandma's room. After a good long rattle of the door knob he flung open the door and switched on the light. Everything was as usual – the framed photographs of Thomas the First, the incense sticks, the books about Breathing. No one had been sleeping in Grand-ma's bed.

'All clear!' he called, and shut the door. He had quite neglected to look either under the bed or in the wardrobe.'

A check of his parents' room, then Rosie's, drew a similar blank. He turned and went back along the landing, passing William, poised for flight at the top of the stairs.

'You're not taking long,' he told Jack. 'Are you doing it properly?'

'I've got Zero,' Jack replied. 'He'll soon sniff anyone out.'

As a matter of fact Zero was now sniffing and snuffing noisily further down the landing, outside the door of Jack's own room.

'Good old Zero!' Jack told him, and followed. As he did so he found himself, too, sniffing. There was a strong odour – or even a mixture of several smells, only one of which he could put a name to – whisky. It was reminiscent of the day Billy Goat Gruff got drunk and destroyed the sitting room. The door of Jack's room was ajar and Zero put up a paw, pushed it and went in. Jack followed.

He took one look, let out a yelp and ran back full tilt, colliding with William, who staggered sideways and himself yelled. Tess, still near the bottom of the stairs, screamed in sympathy, and Rosie started dialling 999.

'No, stop!' cried Mrs Bagthorpe through her tears,

rushing to replace the receiver. 'It may be a false alarm!'

By now Jack, William and Tess were in a tangled heap at the bottom of the stairs.

'What's up?'

'Oh, Jack!' wailed Rosie.

'A man!' Jack gasped. 'On my bed!'

'Dead?' queried Grandma, who had smartly unstretched herself from the sofa at the first sign of action.

'I – don't know!'

'I should think so,' said Grandma with satisfaction. 'No one could possibly sleep through this commotion.'

'The only thing is, there was this smell,' Jack said. 'Of whisky.'

'*What?*'

The study was flung open with a speed that suggested that Mr Bagthorpe had had his ear to it while creating.

'Did you say whisky?'

He was up the stairs, bounding two at a time, before anyone could stop him. It was in any case doubtful that anyone would have tried, even his wife.

The rest of the Bagthorpes huddled at the bottom of the stairs, staring upward.

'My God!' they heard Mr Bagthorpe exclaim. 'Look at that! My best malt – half gone! Wake up, you great brute! D'you hear me, you great stinking evil brute!'

The Bagthorpes, stunned, stared at one another, their worst fears confirmed. Unicorn House did, indeed, harbour a mass murderer. And what was worse, Mr Bagthorpe was trying to wake him up.

3

Mr Bagthorpe failed to arouse the intruder, though it was not for want of violent shaking, and even pummelling. As soon as the rest of the family realized this, they rushed up the stairs to see for themselves. They crowded into Jack's small room and stared down at the old man.

He lay on his back, toes (or rather, boots) turned up, hands on his stomach, and a kind of smile on his face. He looked too old and too fat to be a mass murderer, thought Jack, who in so far as he had ever envisaged this species had always imagined them rather thin, and with narrowed dark piercing eyes. This man's eyes looked as though when opened they would be quite round, and almost certainly blue, given the gingery grey of his stubble. His hair was of uncertain colour. The odd greasy lock visible did not look as if it had seen a shampoo since nursery days, and the rest was hidden by a hat.

'D-d-do you think he's a murderer?' quavered Rosie.

'No, dear,' said Mrs Bagthorpe. 'He appears to be a vagrant, and is almost certainly harmless.'

'Harmless?' echoed her husband. 'Are you mad, Laura? That is twelve-year-old malt whisky he has been gulping down as if it were mother's milk!'

Grandma now appeared in the doorway.

'It is to be hoped that he has not also disposed of the rest of your stock, Henry,' she observed.

At this he clapped a hand to his head, shoved the others aside and raced back downstairs. From the anguished yells that followed his family deduced that the tramp had, indeed, polished off Mr Bagthorpe's considerable reserves of Scotch.

'Pooh! Doesn't he pong!' said Rosie.

'It is a pity that he appears to be a commonplace vagrant,' Tess said. 'If he had been a true traveller, a Romany, I could have carried out some useful research. As a race they have highly developed paranormal powers.'

'Rather your bed than mine,' William said to Jack. 'I bet he's crawling.'

As a matter of fact, Jack felt rather honoured that the visitor should have chosen his own room to kip down in. He had had, after all, plenty of choice.

'He must have thought mine was the best,' he thought with satisfaction.

Jack's was the smallest bedroom in the house. It later emerged that the old boy had picked it as seeming the most like home. It reminded him of the Salvation Army Hostel, he said.

'He can stop here,' said Jack generously. 'Zero and me'll sleep in one of the spare rooms.'

'You haven't got much choice,' William told him. 'Unless you take one end and me the other and chuck him out.'

'That would be most unwise,' said their mother swiftly. 'In his present condition he may be quite belligerent if roused. Our best plan is to close the door and lock it. Then, in the morning, we can decide what is best to do.'

So it was decided. The door of Jack's room was firmly closed, though the key could not be found.

'No matter,' said Mrs Bagthorpe sensibly. 'There is no risk of our being murdered in our beds. He looks rather elderly for a murderer, and will certainly sleep till morning.'

The search of the house was abandoned, as it seemed unlikely that even the Bagthorpes would be entertaining two intruders at once. It was also decided that unloading the luggage could wait until the morning.

This was how Grandpa came to be left out not only in the gathering chill, but also the dew. Later, in one of his rare speeches, he was to say that this was one of the best things that had ever happened to him.

He woke up at around dawn, and could not at first work out why he felt cold. On opening his eyes to find that he was not in bed, but on the back seat of the estate car, he was only mildly surprised. He was, after all, a Bagthorpe.

He climbed out, stretching his aching limbs, and took a few turns along the drive to get his circulation going. He then became aware that he was hungry and thirsty.

He tried both front and back doors. They were locked. Mr Bagthorpe had personally secured them, saying that by now probably every tramp in the neighbourhood thought his home was Liberty Hall. He had no intention, he said, of allowing it to become a doss house.

Grandpa then decided that the only way to get in was to waken one of the household. He had no difficulty in selecting which member. Jack and himself were good friends, and Jack was the only Bagthorpe who was not bad tempered, with the possible exception of Mrs Bagthorpe.

First, Grandpa stood beneath Jack's bedroom window and called his name. This drew a blank. Grandpa did not go in for shouting and yelling as the rest of the family did, and his voice was out of training.

He then hit upon the idea of throwing a pebble up at the window. Later Tess claimed that this, given that he knew nothing of the stones and bricks thrown, or threatened to be thrown, at windows the previous night, proved that he had telepathic powers. Grandma jealously denied this.

'His mind runs along tramlines,' she declared. 'He merely did the obvious. Had *I* been throwing something up at a window, I should have selected something more imaginative. A golf ball, perhaps, or a large potato.'

Grandpa was certainly a better picker of pebbles than his daughter-in-law. He selected a suitable one from the gravelled drive, and tossed it up at Jack's window. At first he had no success. Then, after the sixth or seventh pebble, the window opened, and the head and shoulders of the tramp appeared.

'Morning, mate!'

'Oh! Good morning,' replied Grandpa. He blinked, wondering if his eyesight was going the same way as his hearing. 'I do beg your pardon. I must have selected the wrong window.'

'That's all right, mate,' said the tramp genially. 'Come on in. Liberty Hall this is!'

He guffawed. He had, quite understandably, mistaken Grandpa for a fellow vagrant.

Grandpa was a very unworldly man, and put no store at all by appearances. He took no notice of other people's, and imagined that no one noticed his own. He had been known to enter five star restaurants wearing odd boots and with his trousers held up by an old tie. If he stood around in the street, sometimes people felt sorry for him and gave him money. This surprised him, but he was too good natured to refuse, and usually thanked them politely.

Grandpa was very stubborn about parting with his old clothes. He got fond of them, frayed edges and all. Once, when Mrs Bagthorpe sent a parcel of particularly tattered garments to the Village Jumble, Grandpa padded straight down there on foot and bought them all back. He came home delighted with his purchases.

'I made an excellent bargain,' he told everyone proudly. 'Twenty pence the lot!'

'Then you were had, Father,' Mr Bagthorpe told him. 'You can only have been bidding against a scarecrow. Ha!'

This remark had given him an idea, albeit, as Grandma told him, a very childish and silly one. He raided Grandpa's wardrobe and stole a number of articles, which he then used to dress a scarecrow for the vegetable garden.

Grandpa did not notice for several days, during which there was much heavy rain. When he did, he instantly retrieved the sodden garments and took them to Mrs Fosdyke for drying out.

Mrs Fosdyke reported this incident to her cronies in the Fiddler's Arms with relish.

''E's capable of anything,' she said, meaning Mr Bagthorpe. 'Would you believe – robbing the shirt off his own father's back, and him eighty years old and deaf as a post!'

The latter was not strictly true. Grandpa was SD – Selectively Deaf. This meant that some people he could not hear even when his hearing aid was switched on, and they bellowed into it. These included Mr Bagthorpe, Mrs Fosdyke and his own wife. Other people he could hear perfectly well with or without his aid – Jack, for instance, and most strangers.

The particular stranger now hanging out of Jack's bedroom window and beaming a welcome was perfectly audible to Grandpa. Nor did he see anything untoward in his garb, even the sagging brimmed hat.

'I am afraid the doors are locked,' explained Grandpa apologetically.

'That's rum. They wasn't last night. Least, I think they wasn't. Don't you be worrying. I'll come down.'

The hat withdrew. A minute or so later the front door was open, the tramp and Grandpa stood gazing at one another, and a friendship was born.

Besides omitting to lock the front door and cancel the milk and newspapers, the Bagthorpes, in their excitement about going to Wales, had also neglected to dethaw and empty the fridge (though fortunately the power had not been off long enough for fungus to develop). So when Mrs Bagthorpe came downstairs after an uneasy night dreaming of life without Mrs Fosdyke, it was to find the two old gentlemen tucking companionably into bacon and eggs.

She was startled, but took care not to show it.

'Good morning, Father,' she said. 'Did you sleep well?'

'I believe I did, thank you, Laura,' he replied. 'I usually sleep well in the car.'

'In the—! Oh, how dreadful! Did you really—?'

'It is no matter, Laura,' he told her. 'I am happy, as you know, to sleep anywhere.'

This was true. Mr Bagthorpe often said he could probably sleep on top of a flag pole.

'And what about you, Mr – er—?' she asked.

'O'Toole,' he supplied. 'Joseph O'Toole. And I slept like a top, I'm happy to tell ye. And may I be having the pleasure of hearing your own name?'

'Oh! Bagthorpe. Laura Bagthorpe,' she told him. Then, lamely, 'I live here.'

'And so ye do, I'm sure! I wouldn't be doubting it. And a very fine place ye have, too. I congratulate you, I do indeed.'

'Oh – thank you,' said the bemused Mrs Bagthorpe.

In the intervals between nightmares she had spent the small hours rehearsing a firm magisterial reproof to the intruder. Now, she could not seem to find her cue.

'I spent a very passable night meself, thank you,' Mr O'Toole went on.

'Oh, good. I'm so glad!' said Mrs Bagthorpe. 'Are you ready for toast?'

'I believe I am, ma'am,' came the reply. 'Thanking you kindly.'

Thus Mrs Bagthorpe found herself, instead of lecturing the intruder, making toast for him, and setting out generous supplies of butter and marmalade. This was how her husband discovered her.

He came banging into the kitchen having spent a very bad night with cases of empty Scotch bottles floating before his eyes. He saw the breakfasters and stopped dead.

'What the—? What the blazes is going on?' he demanded.

'Ah, Henry, dear,' said Mrs Bagthorpe swiftly, ever anxious to avoid a scene, if not an affray. 'This is Mr O'Toole. I am just giving him breakfast.'

'So I see,' replied her spouse grimly.

'Good morning to ye, sir,' said Mr O'Toole blithely. 'Will ye not have some toast?'

'And would you believe,' cried Mrs Bagthorpe desperately, 'Father spent the whole night in the car!'

'I do not care where he spent the night!' retorted Mr Bagthorpe. 'I do not care if he spent it on top of a flag pole!'

'I had a very good night,' Grandpa told him. 'Mr O'Toole and I have been having a very interesting conversation.'

'Oh yes?' said his son. 'What about? The price of Scotch?'

'About fishing, Henry,' Grandpa told him. 'Mr O'Toole is very knowledgeable on the subject.'

'I can imagine,' returned Mr Bagthorpe. 'I should think he's poached enough salmon in his time to swim nose to tail down the M1.'

'I have invited him to stay,' went on Grandpa, buttering another piece of toast.

Mr Bagthorpe was not easily floored, but he was now. His face went a deep, suffused pink, his eyes bulged, his mouth opened and shut soundlessly. He himself looked not unlike a beached salmon.

'You – have – *what*?' Eventually he ground out the words.

By then Grandpa and Mr O'Toole had forgotten him and were again deep in conversation about the finer points of fly fishing. Mr Bagthorpe stared disbelievingly for a full minute, then staggered over to his wife.

'Throw him out!' he croaked.

'Certainly not,' replied his wife, who was quite uninterested in Scotch. 'I think it is lovely that Father has found a friend.'

'Friend?' echoed her spouse. 'He's a – a – a hobo!'

'We know nothing about him, Henry,' she replied. 'He may have a very interesting history. Anyone at all might be reduced to his circumstances. You might yourself.'

This he could hardly deny, since he was constantly asserting that his own family were driving him to the brink of penury. Nevertheless he denied it now.

'Bilge!' he told her.

'And his manners are impeccable,' said his wife pointedly.

'Where's *my* toast?' he demanded, snatching a slice from her hand. 'Where's my breakfast? Where's that blasted woman?'

He meant Mrs Fosdyke, whom he took care never to mention by name. He had plenty of names of his own to call her.

At this point Grandma arrived, having spent the

night in deep and dreamless sleep. She took in the situation with a practised eye.

'Good morning, Laura,' she said. 'Good morning, Henry. You look very bad-tempered. I see our visitor is already up. Good morning, Mr – er—?'

'O'Toole, ma'am. Joseph O'Toole.' He rose to his feet, brushing the crumbs from his whiskers with his sleeve. A sure instinct told him that if he was to live the life of Larry at Unicorn House for the next few weeks, Grandma was the one he must win over. Standing, he was an impressive figure, and certainly too big for Mr Bagthorpe to take on. He grinned at Grandma, showing a mouthful of brown stumps and gaps. He drew back his chair and offered it to her with a half-bow.

'Won't ye take me own place, ma'am?'

'Why, thank you, Mr O'Toole,' she replied graciously, and swept forward to take the proffered chair. 'I trust you enjoyed your meal?'

'Oh, entirely, ma'am,' he assured her. 'And the pleasure of conversation with your father, here.'

He meant Grandpa, who was a mere ten years older than his wife. Grandma was enraptured. She prided herself on what she claimed was a remarkably youthful appearance, though no one else could see it. Mr Bagthorpe frequently told her that with her back to the light she might pass as Marlene Dietrich's mother.

'I must correct you,' she now informed Mr O'Toole. 'I fear the gentleman you refer to is my husband.'

She hopefully awaited a gratifying response to this. She was not disappointed. The hobo launched into a string of compliments, while Grandma darted triumphant looks at her son, who was by now on the verge of apoplexy.

'I have invited Mr O'Toole to stay, Grace,' Grandpa told her, when the effusion ended.

'Splendid, Alfred,' she cooed. 'What an original thought! Don't you agree, Henry?'

Mr Bagthorpe's reply, which would certainly not have remotely resembled an agreement, was forestalled by the all too familiar screech of tyres on gravel. The five-star castle in Wales had evidently lost its appeal once the Bagthorpes had left. The arrival of Uncle Parker could not have been better timed if Grandma had cued it herself.

'This will be my son-in-law,' she told Mr O'Toole. 'He has many faults, but is the father of my beloved Daisy. A shining jewel of a child.'

Uncle Parker now breezed in, followed closely by the aforesaid shining jewel of a child, who was in turn followed by Billy Goat Gruff towed by a pink satin ribbon.

'Ooooh, Grandma, darling lickle Grandma Bag!' squealed Daisy, dropping her pet's lead and rushing forward. The pair embraced as though they had been parted for millennia, rather than just under twenty-four hours.

'Hello, all!' said Uncle Parker, taking in the situation at a glance. 'My word, Henry, you look a touch frail. Upset stomach? I see you have ordered sufficient milk to make several gallons of custard. Good idea. Nothing like a bland diet for a weak stomach. Plenty of slops. And lay off the hard stuff for a bit, I should.'

Mr Bagthorpe emitted various groaning noises that might indeed have indicated abdominal pain.

'You have a house guest, I see,' went on Uncle Parker. 'Won't you introduce us?'

Mr Bagthorpe ignored this optimistic request, but his wife stepped swiftly forward.

'This is a friend of Father's, Russell,' she told him. 'Mr O'Toole. Mr O'Toole, my brother-in-law, Russell Parker.'

'Delighted!' exclaimed Uncle Parker, offering a hand to the visitor, who shook it with extreme vigour. Uncle Parker winced, and on withdrawing his hand surreptitiously took the silk handkerchief from his breast pocket, and wiped it.

'A friend of Father's, eh?' he said genially. 'Well, well! At school together, were you?'

'Not exactly, sir, but then again, ye might say we were. Fellow students in the school of life.'

'Splendid!' said Uncle Parker heartily.

Daisy had now disengaged herself from Grandma's embrace and was darting glances about the kitchen with her unnervingly bright eyes. They rested inevitably on Mr O'Toole.

'Who dat funny man?' she squeaked. 'And what dat funny smell? Pooh!'

'That is bacon and eggs, Daisy,' said Mrs Bagthorpe swiftly.

Daisy shook her head vigorously and her Medusa locks and ringlets flew.

'I eated bakeneggs lots of times,' she said. 'What's dat *sniffy* smell?'

She was, as Mr Bagthorpe later pointed out, a fine one to talk about smells. Billy Goat Gruff had a permanent malodorous aura, and resisted all Daisy's determined efforts to bath him. He also, of course, made puddles.

He made one now. He wandered over to Mr O'Toole. He did not exactly wag his tail, but evidently felt some kind of kinship. He sniffed at the tramp's jacket, nuzzled his sleeve, and made a large puddle.

'Look at that!' yelled Mr Bagthorpe. 'Look what that stinking brute's done on my floor!'

'Don't be silly, Henry,' his wife told him. 'There is no carpet to be spoiled.'

She fetched a bucket and mop. She was by now well used to this. Mrs Fosdyke flatly refused to clear up after Billy Goat Gruff, whom she cordially hated. She was often tempted to fetch him a swipe with the frying pan, but never quite dared. He had, after all, twice tried to kill Mr Bagthorpe, or so he claimed.

'Who dat man in the funny hat?' Daisy again demanded. She went right up to him and fixed him with her piercing gaze.

'You all whiskery!' she told him. She put out a

chubby forefinger and poked at his grizzled stubble.

'Whiskery is right!' muttered Mr Bagthorpe. 'Too right he's whiskery!'

'Is oo Forty Feeves?' Daisy mused. 'No, oo an't got no jug to come out of. Is oo a Seven Dwarf? No, oo isn't. Dey lickle – dey lickle like me.'

'It's a fine bright child ye have there,' Mr O'Toole told Uncle Parker.

'I sink you a Hobble-Gobble,' Daisy decided. 'I seed Hobble-Gobbles in my book!'

She dragged up a chair next to him, climbed on to it, and beamed at him.

'I like oo,' she confided. 'Now I got lots of friends. I got Arry Awk and I got Billy Goat Gruff and I got oo!'

'And myself, Daisy!' said Grandma jealously.

'A fine bunch your benighted daughter's got herself mixed up with!' Mr Bagthorpe told Uncle Parker.

'I must say,' said Uncle Parker smoothly, 'that when we all last met here less than a week ago, I hardly thought we should be gathered together again so soon. How long did you book that derelict heap in Wales for, Henry? Six weeks, was it?'

'I'd finished my research!' snapped Mr Bagthorpe. 'I don't go hanging around in idle luxury for weeks on end. I'm a man with a mission!'

Luckily for him, no one asked him what his mission was. He was saved by Daisy, who was again scanning the kitchen with her radar eyes.

'I spy wiv my lickle eye!' she burbled. 'I spy dat der in't no Fozzy! Where Mrs Fozzy, Uncle Bag?'

Mr Bagthorpe groaned.

4

It was only much later that the Bagthorpes learned the facts behind Mrs Fosdyke's mysterious disappearance.

When the two policemen had followed her into her house she had been delighted. She intended to make a lengthy statement about rapers, murderers and the Bagthorpes. She also counted on the police making a thorough investigation of her bed and her wardrobe.

She had been disappointed on both counts. They listened to her rambling version of events, yawning now and again, and frequently urging her to stick to the point. (She usually tried to bring Daisy Parker and Billy Goat Gruff into any statements she made to the police.) Neither of the officers took out his notebook.

'Shouldn't you be taking all this down?' she asked. 'Shall I accompany you to the station?'

'Oh, that won't be necessary, madam,' said One. 'Bit of a storm in a teacup, really.'

Mrs Fosdyke was outraged by this summary of affairs.

'If I'd've been murdered in my bed, it'd've been all over the papers,' she told them.

'Certainly it would, madam,' Two agreed wearily. 'But the eventuality did not arise. Fortunately.'

'It's obvious where he is,' continued Mrs Fosdyke. She lowered her voice. ''E's either under my bed, or in the wardrobe. It's where they always 'ide. Are you going up now, or will you send for reinforcements? I think you should send for reinforcements. 'E's done five in already, remember.'

When it emerged that the police intended to do neither of these things, and prepared to leave, she grew quite desperate.

'Don't go! Don't go!' she pleaded, plucking at One's sleeve. His radio started to crackle and a message came through.

'Sssh!' he told her sternly, yanking his arm free. 'You're obstructing us in the course of our duties.'

'Come on, Mike,' said Two. 'Sounds like trouble at the Three Cups again.'

They went smartly out, leaving Mrs Fosdyke fairly dancing with frustration. She ran to the door and screeched after them.

'I'll report you to the top policeman! Folks that wants to make statements should be *let* make statements!'

They disappeared, and she heard their car start up. She turned back to her suddenly quiet and deserted kitchen. Mrs Fosdyke really did believe that there was someone hiding in her bedroom. She acted fast. Her suitcase stood just inside the door where Mr Bagthorpe had dumped it. Leaving the door wide in case she had to make a hasty exit, she opened the case and rummaged feverishly for her nightie and sponge bag. These she stuffed into a plastic carrier. She switched off the lights, locked the back door and scooted off as fast as her legs would carry her in the direction of the Fiddler's Arms.

There, as she had hoped, she found Mesdames Pye and Bates, hunched over their Guinness in their usual corner. Their astonishment, when their friend threw herself down breathless opposite them, knew no bounds.

'It's Glad!' shrieked Mrs Pye. 'It's Gladys Fosdyke, as ever was!'

'But you're in *Wales*, Glad!' cried Mrs Bates.

Then, in chorus, leaning forward avidly, 'Whatever's 'appened?'

Mrs Fosdyke told them. She did not begin her account until she had knocked back one Guinness almost in a single gulp, and was ensconced behind a second glass.

'Oooh, that's better!' she said. 'Though I'm still all of a tremble. My nerves is in ribbons. I shall 'ave to see the doctor. Last time I—'

'But what 'appened, Glad?' demanded Mrs Pye, who along with Mrs Bates had no interest in Mrs Fosdyke's state of health. She went on a lot about her symptoms in the normal run of things anyhow, blaming most of them on the Bagthorpes. Her cronies had discussed these behind her back, and were agreed that they were all in her mind – psychotic.

'I 'ardly know 'ow to tell you,' she replied. 'I 'ardly know 'ow to start.'

'Start at the beginning, Glad,' suggested Mrs Bates wisely.

And so she did. As she related the horrors of Ty Cilion Duon her friends' eyes widened with disbelief.

'No 'ot water?' cried Mrs Pye. ''Owever did you go on for filling the dishwasher?'

'There wasn't no dishwasher,' Mrs Fosdyke told her. She launched into the dreary litany that had run through her head throughout her stay in Wales. 'No dishwasher, no washing machine, no fridge, no 'oover, no working surfaces—'

'No working surfaces?' shrieked Mrs Bates. ''Ow did you go on for cooking?'

'I ain't finished yet,' Mrs Fosdyke reproved. 'No cooker—'

'No *cooker*?' this in scandalized chorus.

'No cooker,' affirmed Mrs Fosdyke. 'Just one of them 'orrible camping things that blows up.'

'Oooh, did it blow up in someone's face?' exclaimed Mrs Bates. 'Was anyone killed?'

'We all was,' Mrs Fosdyke confirmed. 'We was all nearly killed.'

'Oh – nearly!' Mrs Bates sank back, disappointed.

'I ain't finished yet,' Mrs Fosdyke told her. She sensed that her narrative was not coming up to expectation, and accordingly set about embellishing it. She credited Daisy Parker with having crashed at least eleven police cars, and Billy Goat Gruff with having caused hundreds of thousands of pounds' worth of damage.

'It could even be up to a million,' she asserted.

By now well into her stride, she then launched into a description of the supernatural comings and goings. She upped the number of resident apparitions to a round dozen, and invented a poltergeist.

'Oooh, no!' Mrs Pye shuddered deliciously. 'Not one of them polygamists! I've read about them! They switch the lights on and off and smash all the pots!'

'There wasn't any pots,' Mrs Fosdyke reminded her. 'No pots, no cutlery, no 'oover, no dishwasher—'

'What about the electric, Glad?' interrupted Mrs Bates. 'Did you 'ave electric?'

'Only on and off,' she told them. 'And then 'e started sitting up all night and 'olding these seances.'

'Oooh, 'e never!' Her cronies were enraptured. 'Oooh, that's ever so dangerous, that is, meddling with the supernatural!'

''E didn't even know 'ow to do it proper,' said Mrs Fosdyke scornfully. 'It was lucky I did. It was me that did the polygum and garlic and all that.'

'My sister in Margate once did a seance,' Mrs Bates said. 'She did it with 'er lodger and a glass that goes rushing round the letters of the halphabet. Said it went running round the table like a dodgem car, and scared 'er 'alf to death. Said 'er 'air went white overnight. Some of it, anyhow.'

'We didn't bother with any of that,' said Mrs Fosdyke loftily. She was in danger of being upstaged. 'This was more like out of Dennis Wheatley, with the 'orrible evil powers of darkness, and all that.'

There was still plenty more to tell, and she told it. She was a tireless, if unreliable, chronicler of the Bagthorpe Saga. She described the auction, and how Mr Bagthorpe had bought rubbish worth hundreds of thousands of pounds. She made much of the incident when the Bagthorpes had mislaid Grandpa.

''E could 'ave been laying face down in a foot of water,' she told them. 'And 'im all of eighty-five!'

She seemed to imply that had he been a younger man, he could have survived such an experience with impunity.

'Them Welsh police was disgusted, you could see that. Downright disgusted.'

'It *is* disgusting,' said Mrs Pye.

'Disgusting,' echoed Mrs Bates.

They sat for a moment pondering the extreme disgustingness of the Bagthorpes. Then Mrs Fosdyke realized that her tale had yet to be brought up to date.

'And why do you think I'm 'ere, instead of in me own bed asleep?' she demanded dramatically.

There was a small silence.

'For a drink, Glad?' ventured Mrs Pye.

Mrs Fosdyke shook her head long and hard.

'It's too 'orrible to tell,' she said. 'I think I'd better 'ave another, first.'

Her friends obligingly replenished her glass, and she took sips of it with maddening slowness. She had a very good sense of timing. She could have been a successful dramatist had she had any command at all of the Queen's English.

'It's that mass murderer!' she told them at last in lowered tones.

'Never 'im that done them five women in and got that secret trademark?'

''Im,' nodded Mrs Fosdyke.

She then went on to describe Mr Bagthorpe's lily-livered behaviour in Coldharbour Road, and how he had threatened to heave a brick through her front window. It was lucky that she was blissfully unaware of the gaping hole in her bedroom window caused by Mrs Bagthorpe's accurate aim with a rockery stone.

She went on to describe how even the police had been too frightened to go up to her bedroom.

'It's obvious where 'e is,' she concluded, meaning the mass murderer. 'A child of two could see it. 'E's either under my bed, or in the wardrobe.'

'It does sound like it, Glad,' agreed Mrs Pye dubiously. She herself lived only a few doors away from Mrs Fosdyke, and was beginning to wonder whether she had locked the back door, or left any windows open.

'I shall 'ave to come 'ome with you, Flo,' Mrs Fosdyke told Mrs Bates. 'I've got me things in 'ere.' She indicated the plastic carrier.

'Oooh, it's a bit short notice, Glad,' said Mrs Bates,

whose husband's opinion of Mrs Fosdyke was not materially different from that of Mr Bagthorpe. 'It's a bit short notice.'

'Had to be, Flo,' Mrs Pye told her wisely. 'You don't get a lot of notice, not from murderers.'

'Mass murderers,' corrected Mrs Fosdyke. Then, huffily, 'Of course, if we want me 'atcheted in me own bed and both our names all over the papers . . .'

'Oooh, don't say it, Glad!' shrieked Mrs Bates, a lurid vision of the headlines in her daily tabloid floating before her eyes.

And so Mrs Fosdyke had trotted home with Mrs Bates, leaving the mass murderer thwarted and victimless.

The Bagthorpes, of course, knew nothing of this. So far as they were concerned, Mrs Fosdyke was either lying murdered in her locked house, or had been spirited into thin air. Mr Bagthorpe did not care which of these alternatives proved to be the case, and said so.

'Either way, we're shot of her!' he declared. 'Hallelujah! I never thought to live to see the day!'

'Isn't that a touch short-sighted, Henry?' said Uncle Parker.

'Why?' demanded Mr Bagthorpe. 'Why is it?'

'Because, Henry, Mrs Fosdyke was the pivot on which this household turned. Will you be able to persuade anyone to take her place, I wonder?'

Mrs Bagthorpe turned quite pale at Uncle Parker's use of the past tense. She knew that the possibility of finding anyone local to take Mrs Fosdyke's place was nil. The stories about the Bagthorpes circulated in the village were legion, and verging on the slanderous.

'So what?' retorted Mr Bagthorpe. 'I've had enough of women hedgehogging about with Hoovers to last me a lifetime.'

'Women?' repeated Mrs Bagthorpe sharply. 'Why women?'

He stared at her.

'What's the matter with you? It's women that do all the Hoover-pushing, isn't it?'

'Not necessarily,' she replied. She was about to launch into a speech about sex equality when she realized that she was heavily outnumbered by men. Daisy and Grandma were there, of course, but could not be relied on to back her up. She made a swift mental calculation of the balance of sexes in the family.

'Perhaps yourself and Celia would like to come over for tea today?' she said, and was rewarded by a murderous glare from her husband.

'And darling Daisy could spend the day here with me,' put in Grandma.

'Splendid!' exclaimed Uncle Parker, and left with a suddenness that raised the suspicion that he had only called in the hope of dumping Daisy on to the Bagthorpes.

When the younger Bagthorpes appeared for breakfast they were startled to see that the tramp of the night before was already practically part of the family. By and large they were pleased. They all (except Jack) had very low thresholds of boredom, and Mr O'Toole was nothing if not picturesque. William invited him to look over his radio station in the summerhouse. Tess announced that she would set up tests of his paranormal powers, and Rosie that she would paint his portrait.

'You've got a good face for portraits,' she told him. 'Old people are better than young. You've got really good bags under your eyes and I've never done whiskers before.'

'Before you begin making your plans for the day, I think we should all have a sensible discussion,' Mrs Bagthorpe told everyone. They looked at her uncomprehendingly.

'In the first place, we have no Mrs Fosdyke,' she said. 'And in the second, there is all the luggage to be unloaded. Then, when we have unpacked, I expect there will be several loads of washing.'

'Make me some coffee,' Mr Bagthorpe said. 'I haven't time to waste on this kind of piffling domestic detail. I have serious creative work to do.'

'Don't let him, Mother!' cried Tess.

'He's got more luggage than anybody!' piped up Rosie. 'All those stuffed birds and stags' heads!'

'We will draw up a Plan of Campaign,' said Mrs Bagthorpe. 'And a Rota of Chores. Chores will be evenly divided.'

'Count me out,' Mr Bagthorpe told her.

'I shall do nothing of the kind,' she returned.

'You always get inspired when there's any work to do,' pointed out Rosie, with perfect truth.

'It's almost a law of nature,' Tess contributed. 'Father becomes inspired in direct ratio to the work to be done.'

Her siblings tittered.

'I expect no sympathy and support from my family,' Mr Bagthorpe told them. 'Lord Byron didn't get a lot from his.'

'Would you like me and Zero to go and see if we can sniff out Fozzy?' asked Jack.

'I really see no point at this juncture,' his mother replied. 'Either she has been murdered, or she is having a good lie in after the traumas of the past few days.'

'If that stone you chucked through her window did hit her, she'll have got her worst headache ever,' said Rosie, and giggled.

'This is no laughing matter!' said Mrs Bagthorpe. During the night her worst vision had been of Mrs Fosdyke's waxen face on her pillow, a bloodstained rockery stone lying incriminatingly near by. A forthcoming charge of murder, or at least man-slaughter, seemed all too possible. 'Everyone will be responsible for unloading his or her own luggage,' she said.

'Except myself, of course,' said Grandma. 'Jack, dear, will you be sure to unload my gramophone records carefully, and bring them up to my room?'

'If I see them, I'll smash them,' her son told her.

'I thought that you, Mother, and Daisy, could

clear the table and wash up,' Mrs Bagthorpe continued.

'Oooh, yes!' squeaked Daisy. 'Let's, Grandma Bag! It'll be ever so fun! Can the Hobble-Gobble help?'

Mrs Bagthorpe looked askance. Daisy pointed.

'Oh – Mr O'Toole. Oh – I rather thought that Father might like to freshen up after his night in the car. And perhaps Mr O'Toole also might like to—' she faltered a little '—to freshen up?'

All present held their breaths and prayed for an affirmative reply. The pungency of Mr O'Toole's person was such as to suggest that he had not freshened up in months, if not years.

'I'll surely be taking a little walk, ma'am,' agreed Mr O'Toole pleasantly. ''Tis not often I'm spending the night indoors. The fresh air is the life's blood to me, ye'll understand.'

'Oh – yes, of course,' stammered Mrs Bagthorpe. She had evidently not phrased her question correctly, but had not liked to use the word 'bath' directly. It seemed insensitive.

The next two hours were, even by Bagthorpian standards, chaotic. Six people simultaneously were sorting through the hired van and the estate car, searching for their own possessions and throwing other people's aside with scant respect. Tennis rackets, oil paints, umbrellas and stags' heads flew everywhere. Many of them of course had already been destroyed by Billy Goat Gruff. He evidently regretted having left anything intact, and welcomed the opportunity of rectifying this omission. He now wandered outside and stepped fastidiously among the piles of stuff in the drive, pausing from time to time to chew something, or put a hoof through it.

From the kitchen came the rattle of pots, and now and again a crash, followed by delighted squeals.

By eleven o'clock, when the unloaders gathered for refreshment, tempers were frayed and there were very few pots left. Everyone was constantly tripping over the forest of milk bottles and the purchases made by Mr Bagthorpe at the auction. He had simply heaved them out of the van and dumped them in the nearest available space. When his wife requested that he move them, he refused point blank.

'I haven't decided where to put them. And they need to stop together for insurance purposes. Make things easier for the inspector or assessor or whatever he's called.'

Mr Bagthorpe had never been known willingly to do anything to make things easier for anyone. He did, however, by now believe that the junk he had been landed with was extremely valuable. He had to believe it, for his own self-respect. He also maintained that he liked the stuff, and intended to keep it.

'I have wanted a stag's head ever since I was a boy,' he said. 'And now I have several. I am a happy man.'

'Neither they, nor the stuffed birds, will be put in my dining room or sitting room,' his wife told him. 'They are hideous, and I feel them looking at me with their piercing and dead eyes.'

'Then you are paranoiac,' he told her.

'Oooh, I can see their eyes and they's looking at me!' Daisy now squealed. She went right up to the stuffed birds and fixed them with her own piercing eyes. Then moved on to the stags. She pounced on the scabbiest of these.

'Oooh, a great big Billy Goat Gruff! Where's his poor lickle legs and the rest of him?'

'He is only an ornament, Daisy dear,' Grandma told her. 'Ornaments do not require legs.'

'I sink he's Billy Goat Gruff's grandpa,' Daisy decided. 'Can I have him, Grandma Bag?'

'Of course you can,' Grandma told her.

'At a price,' said her son, making rapid mental calculations.

'Oooh, sank you!' squeaked Daisy. 'Oooh, come on, Grandpa Gruff – I going to call him Grandpa Gruff! Oooh, and look! Der's anunner Grandpa Gruff, and anunner and anunner! Now I got a Hobble-Gobble and lots of Grandpa Gruffs! This is my bestest day ever!'

5

Once the van was unpacked Mrs Bagthorpe announced her intention of driving it into Passingham to return it to the hire firm.

'If you think I'm driving over in the car to bring you back, you're mistaken,' her husband told her.

'I did not dream of any such thing, Henry,' she replied. 'I shall walk back. The exercise will do me good. Tess, Rosie, I should like you to accompany me.'

'Can I come?' Jack asked. In the absence of Mrs Fosdyke meals would undoubtedly be sketchy. He wanted to stock up on private provisions.

'No, Jack,' his mother replied. 'I should like you to stay here and cook lunch.'

Jack boggled.

'To what?'

'Cook lunch. You must use your ingenuity with whatever ingredients are to hand.'

'The boy *has* no ingenuity,' Mr Bagthorpe pointed out. 'Kindly bring me back a pork pie, Laura.'

'Come, Rosie, come, Tess,' she said, and left.

A plan was beginning to form in Mrs Bagthorpe's

mind. This plan would inevitably split the family into two camps. Tess and Rosie were of her own sex, and therefore allies.

'I have been thinking, girls,' she told them, as they wound their way to the village. 'I have been thinking that our family has not altogether moved with the times.'

'I refute that statement, Mother,' Tess said. 'My own investigations into the paranormal are far ahead of the times. I consider myself an innovator.'

'Of course, darling,' agreed Mrs Bagthorpe. 'You are all the time pushing out the boundaries of knowledge, and I am terribly proud of you. What I am referring to is the whole question of sex equality.'

Her daughters stared.

'We are not liberated,' she went on. 'We are still bound by the shackles of outdated roles and stereotypes. You heard what your father said this morning? About hoovering?'

'He said he was sick of women pushing Hoovers around,' said Rosie. 'He meant Fozzy.'

'He meant Mrs Fosdyke,' said her mother, 'but in the absence of Mrs Fosdyke, he meant myself – or you, Rosie, or Tess. Even possibly your grand-mother.'

'Well, *I'm* not pushing Hoovers around,' Rosie told her.

'I'm afraid you may have to,' Mrs Bagthorpe replied. 'Unless we make a concerted stand.'

'Well, I think we ought to go and see how Fozzy

is,' said Rosie. 'She might be stone cold dead from that brick you threw last night.'

'What brick?' Tess demanded.

'Nothing at all,' said Mrs Bagthorpe hastily. 'I merely tossed a pebble at Mrs Fosdyke's bedroom window, and it unfortunately broke the glass. However, perhaps you are right.'

She accordingly turned into Coldharbour Road, albeit with trepidation. As she drew up outside Mrs Fosdyke's residence she looked up and saw that the hole made by her pebble was considerable. She breathed deeply as she climbed down.

'You did *that*, Mother?' exclaimed Tess admiringly, surveying the hole.

'The glass must have been substandard,' said Mrs Bagthorpe. 'It was the merest pebble.'

They found the back door ajar and heard voices within – one of them unmistakably that of Mrs Fosdyke.

'Gladys! Mrs Fosdyke!' shrieked Mrs Bagthorpe.

So powerful were her feelings of relief at finding that she was not, after all, a murderess, that she positively bounded into the kitchen, and there tried to embrace a reluctant and astonished Mrs Fosdyke.

'You're safe and well!' she half-sobbed.

Mrs Fosdyke struggled to free herself from her employer's embrace, while Mrs Bates watched fascinated. She already knew that Mr Bagthorpe was mad, but had hitherto imagined his wife to be comparatively sane.

'She got 'old of Glad,' she later reported to Mrs Pye, 'like as if she was the Prodigal Mother, or something. She knocked 'alf 'er curlers out!'

Mrs Fosdyke extricated herself and took a few scuttling steps away, from which position she eyed the Bagthorpe contingent with suspicion, if not down-right hostility.

'I ain't safe and I ain't well!' she informed them.

'Oh, but *comparatively*, you are!' cried Mrs Bagthorpe. She meant compared with having been hit on the head with a rockery stone.

'I shall 'ave to see the doctor,' Mrs Fosdyke said. 'Flo's going with me.'

'Oh, how kind – Mrs Bates, isn't it?' gushed Mrs Bagthorpe.

'In case I get took dizzy,' went on Mrs Fosdyke, who did not so much have conversations as leave breaks in her monologues where others could chip in if they were lucky.

'I got took terrible dizzy last night, didn't I, Flo?'

'She did,' confirmed Mrs Bates, nodding. 'When we come out of the Fiddler's, it was.'

'We'd have called an ambulance,' went of Mrs Fosdyke, 'only the phone box had been victimized. Them police never searched my premises, you know. I shall write a letter to the top policeman. I could've been murdered in my own bed and all over the papers. Nice thing *that* would've been!'

She clearly thought that she would still be worrying about what the neighbours said after her own demise.

This implied a belief in survival after death. Tess made a mental note to question Mrs Fosdyke about this later.

'She might have had a mystical experience,' she thought, though not with any real conviction.

'There's someone out to get me!' Mrs Fosdyke spoke in a conspiratorial whisper, as if her kitchen were known to be bugged. 'It's 'orrible! 'Orrible! I can't 'ardly tell you – you tell 'em, Flo!'

'There's someone thrown a great big rock in at 'er bedroom window in the night!'

'Oh, how terrible!' said Mrs Bagthorpe faintly.

'Someone must've taken out a contract on 'er,' said Mrs Bates placidly.

'But 'oo, but 'oo?' moaned Mrs Fosdyke, sounding like an owl, rather.

Rosie tried not to giggle, and snorted instead. If a contract had indeed been taken out on Mrs Fosdyke's life, then the prime suspect had to be Mr Bagthorpe, who regularly wished her dead.

'Now I'm sure that no such thing can have happened,' said Mrs Bagthorpe firmly. She knew very well who had thrown the rock, and certainly did not want the police involved. 'You cannot possibly believe that there was a murderer both in your wardrobe and under your bed *and* a murderer outside.'

There she was mistaken. Mrs Fosdyke could, and did. Rosie gave her mother a poke.

'Own up!' she hissed.

Mrs Bagthorpe really had no choice, watched as

she was by her two daughters, both of whom she had counselled from birth always to own up to misdeeds. She drew a breath, a very deep breath.

'As a matter of fact, Mrs Fosdyke dear,' she said, 'there is no cause at all for alarm about the broken window. I myself tossed up a pebble last night, hoping to attract your attention. I shall, of course, immediately arrange for the window to be replaced, and—'

She trailed off, quite unnerved by the expression on Mrs Fosdyke's face.

'You?' she croaked at last. '*You?*'

'You should have seen her,' Rosie told the others later. 'It was just like *et tu, Brute*! I thought her eyes'd drop out, I did honestly.'

'I!' responded Mrs Bagthorpe in ringing tones, entering into the dramatic spirit. 'I, who came back here last night to assure myself of your safety and welfare!'

She omitted to mention Grandma's bladder, which would have added an unwelcome touch of bathos.

'She did,' Rosie chimed in. 'I came with her, and Grandma. 'But you'd already gone to bed, so Mother—'

'I shall 'ave to sit down,' said Mrs Fosdyke, and did so.

'You must not dream of coming in today,' Mrs Bagthorpe told her.

Nothing, it emerged, had been further from Mrs Fosdyke's mind. She intended to visit the doctor, she said, and would not be surprised if he signed her off for weeks, if not months. She might even go and stop with her cousin Doris in Poges, though how much good that would do she did not know, given that Doris dabbled in spiritualism and sometimes held seances at her house. This, of course, stirred the spirits up, and there was the danger that Mrs Fosdyke would herself encounter one and this, she claimed, would probably finish her off. Besides which, Doris could not cook. She could not even stuff an egg.

Somehow the Bagthorpes found an opening in this stream of consciousness and made their escape.

'How fortunate that she is not dead!' exclaimed Mrs Bagthorpe Positively as they drove off up Coldharbour Road, their progress charted by a myriad hidden eyes.

'Very, for you, Mother,' Rosie agreed.

'It certainly appears that she will not be resuming her duties for some considerable time,' said Tess. 'I now begin to comprehend your meaning, Mother, in the matter of sex equality.'

'I intend to introduce the subject as subtly as possible,' their mother told them. 'And I certainly shall not do so as long as we are outnumbered by the opposite sex.'

'Does Mr O'Toole count?' asked Rosie.

Mrs Bagthorpe was inclined to think not.

'But Celia and Daisy certainly do,' she said.

There followed a silence, while Rosie and Tess pondered this. As prospective allies they assessed Aunt Celia as hopeless, Daisy as potentially lethal.

During the walk back to Unicorn House over the fields Mrs Bagthorpe and her daughters discussed their strategy and consolidated their newly formed sisterhood. They arrived home in good spirits and ready for lunch.

'I'm sure Jack will have produced something delicious,' Mrs Bagthorpe said. 'The freezer was very well stocked.'

This, it emerged, was a pity. It would also prove very expensive. It was their luck, as Mr Bagthorpe pointed out, that the large freezer should have been crammed with such delicacies as smoked salmon, Dover sole, prawns and expensive casseroles cooked and frozen by Mrs Fosdyke.

'With any other family there would just have been a few mushy peas in there,' he declared, 'and the odd bag of kippers. Why in the name of all that is wonderful did you turn off the electricity, Laura?'

'Because that is what people do when they go on holiday,' she returned.

'They also cancel their milk and their newspapers,' he told her. 'How come I am faced with an astronomical bill for milk I have never drunk and newspapers I have never read and now salmon I have never ate? Eaten, I mean.'

'If we went away regularly for holidays like any other normal family, then we should be familiar with the necessary procedures,' she countered. 'Your own meanness has now come home to roost, Henry.'

'Certainly it has,' put in Grandma, who had been attracted to the kitchen by the raised voices that signified a Row in Progress.

'Thank you, Mother,' said Mrs Bagthorpe. She made a rapid count. Grandpa and Mr O'Toole were somewhere in the fields, William was in his radio station summerhouse. Mr Bagthorpe and Jack were the only males present, outnumbered two to one, even without Daisy.

'That being so, Henry,' Mrs Bagthorpe went on, 'I think you had better immediately clear the deep freeze.'

There was a silence.

'To – what?' His reactions were those of a man who has been invited to test gravity by leaping into the Grand Canyon.

'I think you heard me, Henry,' Mrs Bagthorpe's heart was hammering, despite her yoga. This was crunch time.

'It's pretty smelly and soggy in there,' Jack said. 'You know – things have gone all slimy.'

'And I expect there will be poisonous moulds growing,' Grandma contributed. 'You had better wear rubber gloves, Henry, unless you wish to risk salmonella poisoning.'

'I have never worn rubber gloves in my life,' replied her son, 'and do not intend to now.'

'Probably a surgical mask too, if we have one,' continued Grandma. 'One never knows what infections there might be, especially with fish. I suspect your resistance to infection is very low, Henry, with your unhealthy life style.'

'I have no time to stand here debating invisible organisms,' said Mr Bagthorpe. 'I'm off to my study. Call me when lunch is ready.'

'No!' Mrs Bagthorpe, Tess and Rosie spoke simultaneously. The effect was arresting.

'You always go sneaking off to your study when there's anything to do!' Rosie told him.

'Certainly he does,' said Grandma. 'He has skulked from childhood.'

Tess had dived into a cupboard and now was holding a pair of pink rubber gloves.

'Here!' She flapped them at Mr Bagthorpe, who backed rapidly off, eyeing them with loathing.

'Is there another pair?' Jack tried to prevent the situation spiralling out of control. 'I'll help, Father.'

Mr Bagthorpe, ignoring this offer, looked at the ring of hostile faces.

'What is this?' he demanded. 'Why am I being victimized?'

'There is no question of victimization,' his wife told him. 'You are merely being called upon to make a contribution to household chores.'

'Household *what*?' exclaimed Mr Bagthorpe in disbelief. He took a final look at them, shook his head and lurched towards the door.

'Stop him, Mother!' cried Tess.

'Stop, Henry!' commanded Mrs Bagthorpe.

'He's doing it *again*!' Rosie screamed. She ran after

him, but Mr Bagthorpe put on a surprising burst of speed and she reached the study door to have it slammed in her face. There followed the sound of the key turning in the lock.

'Come out, come out!' Rosie battered on the door with her fists.

'Go away! I wish to do some serious creative work!'

'Creative work buttercups!' screamed Rosie. She did not know what she meant by this, but she liked the sound of it, and repeated it. 'Creative work buttercups!'

'And you clear off, as well!' she heard her father's voice say. 'Ye gods – where did honour thy father and thy mother get to?'

He was addressing not Rosie but Tess, who had run round the house and was now hammering on the study window and pulling horrible faces.

Mr Bagthorpe felt well and truly cornered, even before he discovered that he had locked himself in along with Daisy and Billy Goat Gruff. Rosie and Tess soon gave up their fruitless hammering (a Bagthorpe never fights a lost cause) and went off plotting revenge.

Mr Bagthorpe heaved a sigh of relief, went to sit at the desk, and his knees encountered something soft – and moving. He let out a yelp and sprang up. There, crouched in the kneehole of his desk, were Daisy and her goat.

'Get out!' he yelled. 'What the blazes are you doing under there?'

Daisy smiled seraphically up at him. She was not afraid of Mr Bagthorpe.

'Hello, Uncle Bag,' she said. 'What all dat banging noises?'

She scrambled out from her hidey-hole, tugging the goat behind her. The creature gazed at Mr Bagthorpe with its clear yellow eyes and chewed meditatively.

'What's that accursed beast chewing?' shouted Mr Bagthorpe.

The goat, clearly more sensitive to noise than its owner, advanced, and Mr Bagthorpe scrambled hastily up on to his chair. He stood there, looking down at the pair of them, feeling extremely silly, albeit relatively safe. He prayed that Tess would not come back to the window and discover him.

'Is oo playing giants, Uncle Bag?' asked Daisy, interested.

'What's that damned animal chewing?' countered Mr Bagthorpe.

He would never, of course, know.

'And what the hell are you doing in here? Get out! Shoo!'

'Billy Goat Gruff and me looking,' Daisy confided. 'We looking everywhere. We looking for a lickle stranger. What *is* a lickle stranger, Uncle Bag?'

Mr Bagthorpe groaned. He began to make wild, clutching movements at his hair, as if trying to tear it out by the roots.

Daisy looked round the room and shook her ringlets.

'I don't sink der's no lickle stranger,' she said sadly.

The door knob rattled violently.

'Henry! Come out this minute!' came Mrs Bagthorpe's voice.

Daisy brightened at this diversion.

'I coming, I coming!' she squeaked. 'Uncle Bag's playing at giants and prisons!'

She scampered to the door. The key turned with ease, owing to its frequent use. The door opened and Mr Bagthorpe leapt smartly down from his chair, though not before his wife thought she had seen him doing so.

'Oooh, Uncle Bag in't no giant any more!' said Daisy treacherously.

'I can hardly believe,' said Mrs Bagthorpe coldly, 'that I am married to a man terrified by a harmless goat.'

'That goat's a killer,' returned her spouse, 'and you know it. I would rather be locked up with a crocodile.'

'Oooh, crockydiles is booful!' burbled Daisy. 'Dey goes tick tock tick tock tick tock and gobbles people up!'

On the whole, Daisy's literary references were more accurate than Mr Bagthorpe's.

'I sink I ask Daddy if I can have a crockydile,' she went on.

'You do that,' Mr Bagthorpe told her. 'With any luck it will see you off – and that stinking goat.'

Mrs Bagthorpe withdrew the key from the lock and pocketed it.

'There!' she said. 'And now perhaps you will go and clear the freezer.'

'I shall start clearing freezers the day hell freezes over,' he told her. 'And wearing rubber gloves.'

She did not reply. Mr Bagthorpe saw that she was looking beyond him at something through the window. He turned to follow her gaze, half-expecting in his present rattled state to see a crocodile.

He groaned. What he saw, more deadly than any crocodile, was an all too familiar scurrying figure rounding the bend in the drive.

'Mrs Fosdyke!' cried his wife. 'Oh, thank heaven, thank heaven!'

'Where that woman is concerned,' said Mr Bagthorpe, 'heaven doesn't enter into it. Not even purgatory enters into it. Where that woman is concerned . . .'

But he was talking to himself.

Mrs Bagthorpe had gone to welcome Mrs Fosdyke back into the bosom of the family and hell, did Mr Bagthorpe but know it, was about to yawn.

6

Mrs Bagthorpe ran through the hall to the kitchen and there she flung open the back door ready to extend an effusive welcome. There was no sign of Mrs Fosdyke. She knit her brow. Her husband, she knew, was quite capable of having rushed to the front door and frightened her off – possibly for ever. As she stood hesitating she heard, at a distance, the dull monotonous tones of Mrs Fosdyke. She was counting.

'Twenty-seven, twenty-eight, twenty-nine, thirty. I don't believe it. I really don't. Thirty-one, thirty-two. I shall wake up soon and find it's only a 'orrible dream. Thirty-three, thirty-four, thirty-five . . .'

Mrs Fosdyke was numbering the milk bottles. Her employer, alarmed at the prospect of her numbering herself into an irreversible trance, ran round the house. (The milkman always delivered to the front door because the rattle of the milk float going past the study window brought a stream of abuse from Mr Bagthorpe, and he had once scattered a bag of nails there.)

She found Mrs Fosdyke slowly passing up the long

line of milk bottles in the manner of one inspecting the guard.

'Forty-two!' She had reached the end of the line and also, it appeared, her tether. 'Forty-two! 'Oo can they've invited to dinner and what are they to eat to use all them bottles? All custards and slops, custards and slops. Pints and pints of custard, gallons and gallons of white sauce—'

'Ah, Mrs Fosdyke, dear!' interrupted Mrs Bagthorpe brightly. 'What a lovely surprise!'

''Oo's coming?' demanded Mrs Fosdyke, dispensing with the niceties. 'Why's there all that milk?'

'No one is coming,' Mrs Bagthorpe assured her. 'At least – only the Parkers, and then only for tea.'

'It's not tea 'e drinks,' said Mrs Fosdyke. 'Not from what *I* hear.'

She was referring obliquely to Uncle Parker's partiality for gin and tonic. She always made such references obliquely, to guard against possible actions for slander. 'And *she* don't drink milk, *nor* tea, nor even proper water!'

She meant Aunt Celia, who sipped only clear bottled spring water.

The third member of the Parker ménage now came skipping round the corner with her pet. Mrs Fosdyke stiffened.

'Ooooh Fozzy Fozzy Mrs Fozzy!' squeaked that infant joyously. She dropped Billy Goat Gruff's ribbons, ran forward and flung her arms round the visitor, at around knee level. This made it almost impossible for Mrs Fosdyke to escape without falling over. She stood helpless, looking down on Daisy Parker's ringlets and bows with unconcealed repugnance.

Rosie, who loved Daisy, said how lovely it was the way she never bore any ill feelings. She forgave people even when they were as horrible to her as Mr Bagthorpe, or Mrs Fosdyke. She said this showed what a truly sweet nature Daisy had. William, who had himself been Daisy's victim in the past, said that it merely showed she had a hide like a rhinoceros.

'That's enough now, Daisy,' Mrs Bagthorpe told her, seeing that Mrs Fosdyke had now shut her eyes, and fearing that she might faint. Daisy abruptly released her hold and Mrs Fosdyke teetered unsteadily, waving her arms for balance. Her gaze went straight back to the milk bottles. She had an obsessive mind – one of the few things she had in common with Mr Bagthorpe.

'That milkman!' she exclaimed. ''E's done this, out of devilment!'

'That is precisely it,' Mrs Bagthorpe said. 'We made a small oversight, in neglecting to—'

'Just let 'im wait!' said Mrs Fosdyke grimly. '*I'll* be ready for 'im!'

This sounded hopeful to her employer. Forty-odd pints of sour milk seemed a small price to pay for a return to duty. She led Mrs Fosdyke round to the back, keeping up a non-stop commentary on how the garden had come on while they were in Wales, in the hope of keeping her mind off other things.

In the kitchen Tess, Rosie and Grandma were talking about Mr Bagthorpe, about whom not one of them had a good word to say. The girls were also trying to fill in Grandma about sex equality and Women's Liberation. This was no easy matter, for the simple reason that Grandma had always had her own way, and had certainly never been exploited by Grandpa. She simply did not know what they were talking about. However she did grasp that what they were outlining was a kind of warfare, against males in general and her son in particular, and this was bound to appeal.

She promised her whole-hearted allegiance to the cause.

'Henry's Day of Reckoning is at hand!' she declared, and itched to deliver the first blow in the coming campaign. Seeing Mrs Fosdyke, she seized her chance.

'Ah, good morning, Mrs Fosdyke,' she greeted her. 'How very timely!'

Mrs Fosdyke looked askance.

'You have arrived just in time to perform the very unpleasant task of clearing out the deep freeze.'

Mrs Fosdyke looked at her bewilderedly. Her mind was still full of milk bottles.

'The deep freeze is filled with mould and fungus and unmentionable germs and bacteria,' Grandma told her, warming to her theme. 'Things are also, Jack tells us, slimy.'

Now Mrs Fosdyke was shaking her head. You could almost hear the milk bottle rattling round in there.

'There's food in the freezer,' she said. 'There's none of it out of date. I label things. I put dates on things.'

'To no avail in this instance, I fear,' sighed Grandma.

'There's smoked salmon, there's fresh salmon, there's Dublin Bay prawns,' Mrs Fosdyke was ticking off the items on her fingers. 'There's two joints of English sirloin, there's two gâteaux I made for that fête and then it got rained off, and there's no end of casseroles. There's Boeuf Bourguignonne—'

'There *are* all those items,' Grandma told her, 'and what an excellent memory you have. But they are now spoiled.'

'Spoiled?'

'Irretrievably,' Grandma nodded. 'My son, who as you know is pathologically mean, switched off the electricity before he went away.'

This was not true. Mrs Bagthorpe had done so, but she let it pass.

'Oh no, oh no!' said Mrs Fosdyke dully. 'Smoked salmon, fresh salmon, Dublin Bay prawns—'

'Exactly!' interrupted Grandma. 'And now a seething mass of mould and fungus!'

The alleged state of the freezer was deteriorating by the minute. It would soon be full of maggots, Mrs Bagthorpe thought, unless Grandma's descriptive flow were curbed.

'It is a terrible shame,' she said, 'and particularly as regards your own casseroles, which are irreplaceable. I could weep.'

This was true. Judging by Mrs Fosdyke's expression, so could she.

'The point is,' went on Mrs Bagthorpe, 'that what is done is done, and there is no point in crying over spilt milk – spilt water, I mean,' she amended hastily, seeing the milk bottles bob to the surface of Mrs Fosdyke's mind again. 'The point is that Henry flatly refuses to clear out the freezer.'

'And defumigate it,' added Grandma, 'and render it sterile. Not a day passes without warnings on the wireless about the dangers of salmonella poisoning.'

Mrs Fosdyke sat abruptly.

'I only came up to get my knitting,' she said.

They all stared at her, thrown by this abrupt tangent.

'Your – knitting, dear?' prompted Mrs Bagthorpe gently.

'Like the doctor told me,' said Mrs Fosdyke obscurely.

Tess and Rosie exchanged raised eyebrows.

''E wouldn't give me any tablets,' she went on. 'Said 'e didn't believe in 'em. And that's a nice thing – what kind of doctor don't believe in tablets? For all I know, 'e don't believe in injections, neither.'

She sat dismally shaking her head.

'But he does believe in – knitting?' said Mrs Bagthorpe.

'Not as such,' Mrs Fosdyke said. ''E says pokerwork would do as well. And Painting by Numbers. And soft toys – ooh, 'e reeled off a great long list, 'e did.'

The Bagthorpes were mystified. Was Mrs Fosdyke finally off her chump, or had perhaps Dr Winters gone off his?

'And origamo, that you do with string,' added Mrs Fosdyke. 'It's all instead of tablets. Occasional Thurpy it's called.'

'Oh, I see!' exclaimed Mrs Bagthorpe, mightily relieved.

'Perhaps clearing out the deep freeze would qualify as Occupational Therapy,' Grandma suggested, keen to keep that topic on the boil.

'What a sensible idea!' cried Mrs Bagthorpe.

If Mrs Fosdyke could be persuaded to regard household duties as Occupational Therapy, then the present crisis would be resolved. But Mrs Fosdyke was already shaking her head.

''E never said anything about freezers,' she said. Then, as an afterthought, 'Cooking was on the list.'

Mrs Bagthorpe seized this straw.

'Of course! Cooking is highly creative – *very* Occupational Therapy! Oh, what excellent news. I'm sure Dr Winters is quite right, Mrs Fosdyke dear. Cookery is much better for you than tablets, which can sometimes have quite dreadful side-effects.'

Mrs Fosdyke regarded her suspiciously.

''E never said anything about 'oovering, and washing and ironing and dusting and—'

'Of course not! You should only gradually return to the rest of your duties. But I'm sure you should take the doctor's advice and cook!'

There was a pause during which all present, including Grandma, held their breath.

'And knit,' said Mrs Fosdyke at last. 'That's what I come up for – my knitting.'

She got up and went unaccountably to the fridge. She opened the door and peered in, sniffing noisily.

''As 'e turned this off as well?' she demanded.

'Henry has turned off everything,' Grandma told her.

'If it's been turned off and then on again it'll 'ave to be turned out thorough and cleaned,' pronounced Mrs Fosdyke. 'It's to be 'oped my knitting'll still be cold.'

She foraged about and withdrew a plastic bag through which could be discerned knitting pins and wool of an unattractive salmon shade.

'What an original idea!' said Mrs Bagthorpe faintly. 'To keep one's knitting in the fridge, I mean.'

'I thought of it meself,' Mrs Fosdyke told her smugly. 'It's a boon in 'ot weather. I fair detest sticky pins!'

'Oh, so do I!' agreed Mrs Bagthorpe fervently.

Mrs Fosdyke stowed her refrigerated knitting in her bag.

'Did you say them Parkers is coming for tea?' she asked. 'I shall 'ave to check me ingredients.'

Under the relieved gaze of the assembled Bagthorpes she took the knitting out again, put it back in the fridge, hung her bag and cardigan on the knob on the back door and began to hedgehog about the kitchen in her accustomed manner, opening cupboards, peering in bins and thoroughly occupied. Her Occasional Thurpy had begun.

'What about the deep freeze?' demanded Grandma.

Mrs Bagthorpe frowned at her. Mrs Fosdyke appeared not to have heard.

'Tess! Rosie!' hissed their mother. 'Go and find Jack and William! I want them immediately!'

She had decided that she would, for the time being, compromise. The boys would clear and clean the freezer and fridge. A shouting match with Mr Bagthorpe at this juncture could easily send Mrs Fosdyke scooting off home again with her refrigerated knitting.

Jack and William were so overjoyed to hear that Mrs Fosdyke was to stay and cook that they agreed to the cleaning of the fridges with good grace.

'I will drive into Aysham and buy everything needful to restock it,' their mother told them. 'So be sure it is done when I return.'

Grandma, fuming because her son was still holed up in his study, announced her intention of playing her records of Wagnerian opera. That, if anything, should flush him out, she thought with satisfaction. First she went in search of Daisy, whom she eventually tracked down in amongst the shrubbery with Billy Goat Gruff.

'I'se getting tired of looking and so's Billy,' Daisy confided. 'What does a stranger look like, Grandma Bag?'

'We do not know what a stranger looks like by definition, Daisy darling,' Grandma told her. 'We only recognize him by *not* recognizing him.'

There was silence while Daisy chewed over the complicated metaphysics of this statement.

'But in any case, Daisy, you are never, ever to go with one. And you must never ever even speak to one, or accept sweets from him.'

'Has strangers got sweets, den?' inquired Daisy, brightening somewhat.

'All too often,' said Grandma darkly. 'And you must never ever accept one. You may rely upon myself for all the sweets you will ever need. Now come along with me, and we will play my gramophone records.'

Daisy skipped along with her willingly enough. She was no devotee of grand opera, but knew from experience that Grandma was usually where the action was. And Daisy liked, above all things, action.

'Never ever never ever!' she warbled merrily as she went, Billy Goat Gruff, as ever, in tow. 'Never ever never ever! Tirra lirra by the river!'

Mr Bagthorpe, hunched in his study, was having a poor creative morning of it. No sooner had the Valkyries set up their caterwauling at full volume in Grandma's room, than Tess and Rosie set up in competition, on oboe and violin respectively. Both instruments had been seriously impaired by Billy Goat Gruff and their counterpointed sounds were excruciating. They could not be blotted out even by the ear muffs Mr Bagthorpe kept in his desk drawer for such contingencies.

'Hell's bells!' he muttered, and it seemed to him that he was already hearing these.

Meanwhile, his elder son was also hearing warning bells ring.

'I think you and me have got to watch it,' he told Jack, as they heaved sodden and stinking masses of delicacies into dustbin bags.

'Why have we?'

'I think there's something afoot. I think Mother's up to something.'

'Oh, I shouldn't think so,' said Jack, who was an optimist, despite the mayhem and disaster he had witnessed over the years.

'Why aren't Tess and Rosie helping with this disgusting mess?' said William. 'Why did Mother take them with her to the village, and not us? I think she's got it in for us, for some reason.'

'I think Mother likes me,' said Jack simply.

William gave him a pitying look.

'Well, you suit yourself,' he told him. 'I'm going to lay a few foundations. I think I might be going to develop a mysterious and debilitating illness. You know what a hypochondriac Mother is.'

Jack didn't. He didn't even know what hypochondriac meant, or debilitating either, for that matter.

'Then I could be put in isolation for fear of infection,' William continued. 'I could have my camp bed in the summerhouse. I've lost touch with a lot of my contacts, being in Wales.'

'What about Anonymous from Grimsby?' Jack asked.

'Not a peep,' William told him bitterly. 'I've just thought. If you were ill as well, it would be better. Then Mother'll think it's some infection we've picked up from this revolting lot. Serve her right.'

'I'll think about it,' Jack promised. 'What about Zero, though? I don't think he'll be able to act ill.'

William surveyed Zero, who was slumped at a distance, evidently made nervous by the pungent smells from the freezer.

'If you ask me, he needn't act any different from usual,' William said. 'He looks half dead at the best of times.'

In the kitchen Mrs Fosdyke was planning the menus for lunch and tea. She hated waste. She was capable, Mr Bagthorpe said, of re-heating a half-eaten jelly. She certainly intended to incorporate as much milk as possible into her dishes. With this in mind she trotted round to the front of the house with two large carrier bags to bring the milk in. She stopped and stared.

'That's funny . . .' she said. 'There don't look as many as there was, to me. Was I seeing double? Could've been, I s'pose, the state my nerves is in.'

She decided that this must be the case, and filled her bags with bottles from the far end of the queue, as being the freshest.

'Come to that,' she asked herself, ''oo'd go pinching bottles of curdled milk?'

The answer to this was Daisy Parker.

Mrs Fosdyke decided that the Bagthorpes would have porridge for lunch, followed by bread and butter pudding with a good thick layer of custard on top.

'That'll see off five pints,' she thought with satisfaction. 'And they can all 'ave milk to drink with their meal instead of water. And there's one extra, so that'll 'elp.'

She meant Daisy Parker, who only under these exceptional circumstances would Mrs Fosdyke have ever described as being a help. She did not, of course, know about Mr O'Toole. Nobody had thought to warn her, and in any case by now most of the Bagthorpes had forgotten about him, relentlessly self-absorbed as they were.

Grandpa and his new-found friend had spent the morning happy in one another's company and planning fishing trips to come. At around noon, as they sat on a bench by the river, Grandpa dozed off. Mr O'Toole decided to set off back to Unicorn House alone. He thought that perhaps his hosts were in the habit of taking a pre-lunch drink, and was inclined to join them.

As he entered the kitchen Mrs Fosdyke, her bread and butter pudding safely in the oven, was in the larder foraging for porridge oats. She turned back, clutching a packet in each hand, and came face to face with the tramp.

Mrs Fosdyke's heart, she later claimed, actually stopped beating.

'It just stopped,' she told the enthralled Mesdames Pye and Bates. 'I could *feel* it stop. I was as good as dead on me feet.'

Be that as it may, Mrs Fosdyke, faced by the mass murderer of her nightmares, wasted no time waiting for her heart to start up again.

She emitted a piercing shriek (likely to attract nobody's attention, given the racket on the upper floors), dropped the oats, and ran. It was a measure of her desperation that she ran out of the kitchen into the hall and then into Mr Bagthorpe's study.

Mr Bagthorpe was sitting at his desk doodling with figures, working out what kind of price he could charge Uncle Parker for Daisy's stags' heads. Hearing the door burst open behind him he whirled round.

On seeing Mrs Fosdyke, her eyes popping like a landed fish, mouth opened for another scream, it is likely that his own heart stopped beating. She uttered a shuddering moan, then turned and slammed the door shut behind her. She leaned her back against it, breathing heavily and staring wildly into the eyes of her old adversary.

The scene had an air of surrealism. Mr Bagthorpe honestly did not believe what was happening. He half-expected the ground to open under his feet. He felt himself to be on the very brink of the pit.

He must save himself. He hastily averted his eyes

from Mrs Fosdyke's mesmerizing glare. He could not stand looking at her at the best of times.

'Oooooh!' she moaned. 'Oooooh!'

'Get out!' he yelled. 'Quick! Get out!'

Mrs Fosdyke's knees bent. She slithered down against the door and sat with a bump. Above her rasping breath came the mingled strains of oboe and violin and the fractured Vienna State Opera Company. The end, so far as Mr Bagthorpe was concerned, was nigh.

He was torn between the urge to drag her out of the way and escape, and an equally strong antipathy to the very thought of touching her. He had never touched Mrs Fosdyke and the thought of doing so now filled him with an almost superstitious dread.

What he did in the end was what he would have done in the event of fire (or in the event of a mass murderer coming at him with an axe). He ran to the window, flung it open, scrambled on to the sill and dropped into the rose bed, scratching himself severely in the process. He then ran round the house to re-enter by the kitchen, not knowing that it contained a mass murderer. He arrived just in time to find Mr O'Toole helping himself to a liberal measure of Scotch.

'Cheers!' he remarked pleasantly. 'Pour you one, shall I?'

He evidently took Mr Bagthorpe's strangled croak as an assent. He poured an equally stiff measure and handed it to his host, who seized it wordlessly and downed it in a single gulp.

'Cheers!' said the tramp again, mildly reproachful at this failure in good manners.

At this juncture Mrs Bagthorpe returned from Aysham with her haul of frozen food.

'Mrs Fosdyke!' she called as she opened the door and caught the delicious scent of bread and butter pudding. 'Oh – it's you, Henry. Oh – Mr O'Toole! Where is Mrs Fosdyke?'

'That woman', her husband told her, 'is in my study. She's raving mad. She's in a heap on the floor. I want her out – fast!'

Uttering a low cry Mrs Bagthorpe hurried from the room.

'Would that be the lady I saw as I came in?' asked Mr O'Toole. 'I fear I startled her.'

Mrs Fosdyke was at that moment still on the floor in the study, cradled in her employer's arms and rambling incoherently about a mass murderer with a beard.

'There there, hush now,' Mrs Bagthorpe soothed. 'It was only Mr O'Toole. He's a friend of Mr Bagthorpe senior, and as harmless as a kitten.'

Grandma, who had come down to discover the effect of her Wagnerian concert on her son, now peered round the door.

'Where is Henry?' she asked. 'What are you doing down there, Mrs Fosdyke? Has he assaulted you?'

Mrs Fosdyke, by now somewhat restored, told her.

'Henry's behaviour is quite disgraceful,' Grandma said. 'He left you lying there for dead while saving his own skin.'

'Though Mr O'Toole is perfectly harmless,' put in Mrs Bagthorpe hastily. 'There was no real cause for alarm.'

She felt that she must paint the visitor in as rosy a light as possible before Mrs Fosdyke caught a whiff of him.

'He is a perfectly charming man,' Grandma confirmed. She had her own reasons for wishing Mrs Fosdyke to accept the tramp into the household. 'Though a trifle eccentric. He is an old friend of Alfred's.'

''E didn't look it,' said Mrs Fosdyke dubiously.

'He is an eccentric millionaire,' said Grandma recklessly. 'Apparently he scatters bundles of ten-pound notes everywhere he goes.'

'Really?' Mrs Fosdyke perked up at this.

'He likes to pretend he is a tramp,' continued Grandma, warming to her theme, and ignoring her daughter-in-law's open mouthed amazement at this string of falsehoods. 'Apparently this is quite common with multimillionaires. They wish to be accepted for themselves, and not just for their money. I think it quite understandable. I am often tempted to do the same myself.'

'Well . . . if 'e's a friend of Mr Bagthorpe senior's . . .' Mrs Fosdyke's milk bottles had at a stroke been replaced by bundles of tenners.

7

The Bagthorpes did not find being served porridge as first course for lunch particularly remarkable. They had eaten stranger meals in their time. They simply wolfed it down with lashings of brown sugar and cream, and looked forward to the pudding to follow.

Mr O'Toole, made mellow by his pre-prandial Scotch, was fulsome in his praise. Having got Grandma in his pocket, he was now out to woo Mrs Fosdyke.

When that lady had been led back into the kitchen earlier, Mr O'Toole had actually bowed to her, which immediately reassured her because she had not read anywhere that mass murderers bowed to their prospective victims. She very nearly bobbed a curtsey in return. He had then launched into earnest apologies for having startled her earlier, ending with the plea, 'Will ye forgive me? Will ye?'

Mrs Fosdyke, who had never before been begged forgiveness in so direct a manner, coyly said, 'I do!' Upon this he had advanced, towering over her, picked up one of her nerveless hands and kissed it, or at any rate brushed it with his whiskers.

'Ye're a true lady, I see it at a glance,' he told her.

Mrs Fosdyke could not but be pleased by this, particularly coming from one whom she knew to be a disguised millionaire who must mix daily with lords and ladies. She did, however, catch a powerful whiff of his person as he made the flourish.

'Poor old gentleman,' she thought. 'Fancy a millionaire like 'im 'aving to go without 'is baths to make sure people aren't after his money!'

She rewarded him with a twisting of the mouth that quite startled him. Mrs Fosdyke found it an effort to smile, and it showed.

He was now loud in his praise of first her porridge and then her bread and butter pudding, of which he had three helpings, to the disgust of Mr Bagthorpe, who would dearly have liked more himself but was certainly not going to ask.

'I expect your cooks must come and go, Mr O'Toole,' Grandma said.

'Ah, they do indeed,' he sighed, thinking she meant the volunteers who doled out noodle soup and stew at the Salvation Army. 'A cook of the genius of this lady here must be worth a king's ransom!'

Mrs Fosdyke glowed and expanded and bundles of tenners rose again before her eyes.

'If 'e asks me to go and cook for 'im, I shall,' she later told her cronies in the Fiddler's Arms. ''E said my bread and butter pudding was a foretaste of 'eaven.'

'Ooooh – I bet none of them others never says anything like that!' said Mrs Pye, meaning the Bagthorpes.

'They 'aven't got the language,' Mrs Fosdyke told her. ''E's got the most beautiful way with words.'

'That'll be on account of 'is being a millionaire,' said Mrs Pye knowledgeably.

'Oh, it will be,' agreed Mrs Bates. 'I expect 'e's got a lot of yachts?'

'Bound to 'ave,' said Mrs Fosdyke carelessly. ''E 'asn't mentioned them, but that's understandable.'

'What does 'e look like, Glad?' asked Mrs Pye.

'Well, o' course 'e dresses like a tramp,' she said, 'like I told you. But 'e's ever so tall and distinguished-looking. Oh, you'd pick 'im out in a crowd, all right!'

This was certainly true – unless, of course, the crowd happened to be one at the Salvation Army.

Mr Bagthorpe sat moodily through lunch, feeling cornered and persecuted. He wondered what he could have done to deserve having both Daisy Parker and Mr O'Toole at his table. He would never, in a million years, have invited either of them. They, on the other hand, appeared the happiest people present, though Grandma kept giving a secret smile that he didn't much like the look of. Grandma and Mr Bagthorpe rarely smiled at the same things.

Daisy was enchanted with the Hobble-Gobble and had insisted on sitting next to him. Jack, who was opposite, supposed that living in the company of Billy Goat Gruff must have inured her to strong smells.

'My mummy coming soon,' Daisy told Mr O'Toole. 'My mummy likes Hobble-Gobbles.'

This Jack doubted. He thought Aunt Celia would

probably take one look – or sniff – at the tramp and swoon clean away. The look of grim satisfaction on Mr Bagthorpe's face seemed to indicate that he was thinking much the same thing.

The meal over, the matter of clearing the table and washing up arose.

'I'm off,' said Mr Bagthorpe, and was, before anyone could stop him.

'I'll be glad to do it meself,' offered Mr O'Toole gallantly. 'I'd count it an honour to be washing up after such a meal.'

Mrs Fosdyke simpered horribly.

The tramp, however, did not even know what a dishwasher looked like, let alone how to use one. Mrs Fosdyke saw at once that this was bound to be the case.

'Bless 'is 'eart!' she thought uncharacteristically as he put a fistful of cutlery on to the top rack and it fell straight through to the bottom. She went and showed him how the various dishes were stacked, and the pair of them ended up happily doing it together, which suited the Bagthorpes.

'When the dishes are done I shall require you, Jack, and you, William, to lay the table for tea,' Mrs Bagthorpe told them. 'We shall have it in the dining room.'

'There you are!' said William to Jack, *sotto voce*. '*Us* again.'

'Mr O'Toole and myself are going fishing,' Grandpa said. 'Will there be stuffed eggs at tea?'

'Of course there will!' cried Mrs Fosdyke generously.

'You'll like them,' Grandpa told his new friend. 'Mrs Fosdyke does the most splendid stuffed eggs.'

Mrs Fosdyke had not blushed so much in years. She made a flask of tea for the two fishermen and waved them off at the door.

''Appy 'unting!' she called after them as they ambled off together.

Mr Bagthorpe, skulking in his study, heard this valediction and took it to mean that the danger of being involved in washing up was now over. Still he could not settle. He hoped he was not going to have another block.

'I can't afford one,' he thought. 'Not after that Welsh fiasco.'

He tried all his usual ploys to woo inspiration. He got up and roamed about the study, peering at the framed stills from his past TV programmes, fulsomely signed by the actors involved. 'To Henry Bagthorpe with deepest admiration – Michael Hordern.' 'To dear Henry with love – Hannah Gordon.'

None of this gave him much comfort. Not even a photograph of a well-known actor in a feather head-dress reading Mr Bagthorpe's adaptation of *Hiawatha* for a recent *Jackanory* comforted him. He could remember only too clearly the words of one reviewer, who wrote that Longfellow's verse and Henry Bagthorpe's prose had as much in common as the song of a nightingale and that of a parrot, and suggested that *Jackanory* should have got a parrot to do the reading.

He then pulled out a scrapbook of reviews and other press cuttings. This was a more satisfactory exercise, since Mr Bagthorpe kept only the good ones. Bad ones he would toss into the waste bin, saying, 'Reviewers killed John Keats. They are not going to kill me.'

Still Mr Bagthorpe could not settle to any serious creative thinking.

'I need calming down,' he told himself. 'I'll go and Watch Goldfish.'

He found that Watching Goldfish helped the creative flow. When the garden pool had been excavated and stocked the previous year at enormous expense, he had claimed the cost against income tax. The Tax Inspector had first queried this, then disallowed it. Mr Bagthorpe had been furious. He had rung the Inspector and yelled at him over the telephone. He made a lengthy speech about the hopelessness of the Inland Revenue's ever understanding the working of a serious creative mind, and about how lucky it was that Shakespeare and Keats had never had to fill in tax forms.

'The world would have lost *Hamlet* and *Endymion* and the lot,' he told the bemused Inspector. 'And if Tax Inspectors spent more time Watching Goldfish the country would not be in the state it now is!'

Mr Bagthorpe cautiously opened his study door, and decided to nip out at the front rather than risk going through the kitchen. Once outside in the warm sun, he strolled past the line of milk bottles in the direction of the pool, already feeling calmer at the very thought of Watching Goldfish.

This calmness was to be short lived. He went through the rose garden and on to the stone terrace beyond and paused to enjoy his first view of the pool.

He stared. Ranged round the pool at random intervals were a large number of empty milk bottles. (Twenty-three, it later emerged.)

Mr Bagthorpe, his calmness already displaced by dark premonitions advanced slowly, still staring, trying to work out the implications of twenty-three milk bottles by the pool. Nobody could possibly have sat there Goldfish Watching and drunk that amount of milk, especially as it was undoubtedly curdled. Besides, nobody but himself went in for this activity. The Bagthorpes had better things to do than Goldfish Watching, which could not possibly count as a String to anybody's Bow.

Then Mr Bagthorpe saw where the milk had gone. The usually clear, greenish water was now thick and cloudy. Curdled yellow flecks floated on the surface and coated the leaves of the lilies. Here and there floated a dead goldfish, pale underbelly upturned. Goldfish Watching, for Mr Bagthorpe, was clearly out, and would be for many a long day.

He clenched and unclenched his fists, and throwing

back his head like an animal howled: 'It's that bloody infant! I'll kill her! I'll kill her!'

He swung round and raced back towards the house, intent on carrying out this threat. His hands made involuntary strangling motions as he went. They itched to twist that ringleted head on its plump white stalk till it came right off.

Whether or not he would have strangled Daisy Parker had not fate intervened will never be known. Mr Bagthorpe himself ever afterwards maintained that he would.

'And I'd have been let off with a caution,' he averred. 'Justifiable homicide. The law in this country is no ass.' (This was not what Mr Bagthorpe usually said about the law. Usually he called it things very much less flattering than an ass.)

In the event Mr Bagthorpe was prevented from strangling Daisy Parker by the arrival – fortuitous or not, depending on how you looked at it – of her parents. Uncle Parker's car shot up the drive grazing the remaining milk bottles and nearly running down Mr Bagthorpe himself, who was just bursting out of the shrubbery. Yelling and shaking his fists he chased after the car and arrived, redfaced and panting, just as Uncle Parker nimbly leapt out and went round to help his wife. He looked, as always, cool as a cucumber – in marked contrast to his brother-in-law.

'Hello, there, Henry!' he greeted him. 'Just back from a jog?'

This was said with intent to infuriate. Uncle Parker

was well aware of Mr Bagthorpe's views about physical exercise in any form. He could not be persuaded even to watch sport, let alone participate in it. For joggers he had especial contempt, and would often hoot and jeer at them as he went past in his car, deliberately driving through puddles to splash them. One reason for this was that he had a conviction that most joggers were bank managers.

'You can tell by their faces,' was all he would say when challenged to justify this. 'You can tell by their hair – or rather the lack of it. Ha!'

He was not aware that Uncle Parker rose at six o'clock every morning to jog, nor did Uncle Parker intend that he should ever discover this. He carefully cultivated an image of being laid back and suave, which fitted ill with jogging. There was little danger of Mr Bagthorpe finding out because he rarely rose before half past eight when the postman came.

At the present moment Mr Bagthorpe was too out of puff to confide to Uncle Parker that he was on his way to murder Daisy.

'So you're a closet jogger, eh?' went on Uncle Parker blithely. 'Well, well! We're a touch early for tea, I know. The thing is, Celia is feeling a trifle fraught.'

'When – is she – not?' gasped Mr Bagthorpe.

'When she's like this she usually winds down by gazing at the fountain in the pool,' Uncle Parker went on. This, given her brother's penchant for Goldfish Watching, suggested a strong hereditary trait. 'The trouble being that Daisy's bunged the thing up with wax or nail varnish, or something. So I thought I'd bring Celia over to gaze at yours.'

'The plashy pool,' murmured Aunt Celia. 'The glassy green translucent wave . . .'

Mr Bagthorpe was in possession of the certain knowledge that there was little glassy green or translucent about the waves in *his* pool. He kept this to himself. Postponing the strangulation of Daisy till later, he decided to give the pair a head-start, then follow them.

'I can then watch Celia swoon into that hellish brew,' he thought. 'I can watch her drown in that curdled broth of her daughter's making. That'll be poetic irony, if you like!'

This he accordingly did. The Parkers wound their languid way through the garden, and Mr Bagthorpe stalked them at a distance which he narrowed gradually, because he wanted to have a good view of what happened.

Judging by the abrupt halt he came to, Uncle Parker was first to spot that something was amiss. He reached for the arm of his wife, evidently with the intention of drawing her away from the ghastly sight, but too late.

Mr Bagthorpe, crouched among the hybrid tea roses, saw his sister's hand fly to her lips and heard the faint cry as she began to sway, as he had hoped, on the brink of the pool.

'There she blows!' he told himself delightedly.

Uncle Parker fielded his wife very neatly, but

in doing so came very near keeling over into the pool as well. This, of course, would have made Mr Bagthorpe's day. He might even have let Daisy off her death sentence. As it was, neither of them went in, though Aunt Celia appeared to have gone into a particularly heavy swoon. Mr Bagthorpe watched Uncle Parker laying her on the warm grass and bending tenderly over her, chafing her wrists.

'What a fool the man is!'

Mr Bagthorpe was disgusted. He certainly would not himself have risked a ducking to save his own wife from toppling into the pool. On the contrary, he would probably have laughed. As she shook the curdled yellow globules from her face and hair he would probably have come up with a quip about Cleopatra and asses' milk. There again, Mrs Bagthorpe was not much given to fainting. If ever she felt the temptation, she Breathed.

No longer able to bear looking at all this marital soppiness Mr Bagthorpe turned and set back to the house to murder his niece. He was uneasily aware that the urge to do so had been somewhat dissipated by the delay, and was now worried that he might not be able to do it.

'I am, after all, a mild man,' he told himself.

It was, then, something of a relief when emerging on the drive he saw two figures approaching at a fair lick. They were those of Grandpa and Mr O'Toole, the latter dripping wet. He had fallen into the river. Mr Bagthorpe showed scant sympathy.

'No real danger of pneumonia,' he said. 'Not with all that Scotch inside you.'

'Just as I was saying,' said Grandpa. 'What he needs is a good stiff Scotch.'

Mr Bagthorpe hurried on ahead to hide his one remaining bottle. It was still in the kitchen, and Mrs Fosdyke gave him a very funny look when he whipped it up and made for his study.

''E's took to drinking in the afternoons now,' she would later tell her friends in the Fiddler's Arms. 'And of course, when that poor old millionaire gentleman come in soaking wet and 'is teeth fairly chattering, there wasn't a drop to be 'ad. Lucky there's a bottle of brandy I keep 'id for my cooking, so I give 'im a nip of that.'

The nip, in fact, was something like a pint.

As Mr Bagthorpe later pointed out, he probably needed the Dutch courage at the prospect of taking a bath. This Mrs Fosdyke hastily ran for him, with generous lashings of expensive bath oil Mr Bagthorpe had been given for Christmas and was saving, he said, for a special occasion.

'Soon as you get them wet things off, you just throw 'em out 'ere, on the landing,' Mrs Fosdyke told the quaking Mr O'Toole. 'I'll soon 'ave 'em dry for you.'

She was going to shove the whole lot in the washing machine. She was going to have her resident millionaire clean and sweet smelling, however eccentric. She felt in the pockets before doing so.

She found old gloves, plugs of tobacco and half-eaten buns, but no bundles of tenners.

What actually happened to Mr O'Toole during the hour he spent in the bathroom, nobody knew. Whatever it was, it was in the nature of a conversion, a baptism, even. The old man had never had a piping hot bath before, or at least not in his memory. At first he was understandably nervous. However he decided to treat the experience as just one more challenge such as he often met in a life on the road, and climbed in.

There followed an hour of pure bliss. He lay up to his chin in the water, topping it up from time to time. He felt free and floating as never before. (He had also, of course, just drunk a pint of brandy.) As he lay there he resolved to take a hot bath every single day thereafter – two a day, even. In days to come, long queues would form outside the Bagthorpes' bathroom.

Now and then Mrs Fosdyke would come and tap on the door and inquire if he was all right.

'Perfectly, dear lady, perfectly,' he intoned each time.

Mrs Fosdyke was enchanted. Even when she saw the layer of sludge left in the bath when the plug was pulled out, she was enchanted. As one who was herself addicted to the ritual of the bath, with all its attendant pink candlewick and scented salts, she was now inclined to think Mr O'Toole not only eccentric, but a saint.

''Ow 'e must've suffered!' she thought pityingly.

When the tramp finally emerged, draped in a bath sheet, there arose the problem of what he was to wear while his own clothes were being laundered. Nothing belonging to Grandpa or Mr Bagthorpe would fit. This was just as well, because the latter would certainly have refused point blank to lend anything.

However his wife, who was much given to the ethnic, came up trumps with a large, sarong-type garment which, however many times she wrapped it round herself, still tended to trip her up. It was of deep purple, with a design in orange and white. It was passed through the bathroom door and Mr O'Toole arranged himself in it.

When he emerged he was a truly impressive figure.

'Oooh, you look just like an emperor!' cried Mrs Fosdyke admiringly. 'As ever was you do!'

'Wonderful!' agreed Mrs Bagthorpe, clasping her hands. 'You must keep it, Mr O'Toole! No, really, I insist. I hardly ever wear it, and it suits you so marvellously well!'

It was by now teatime, and the Bagthorpes and their visitors foregathered in the dining room. Aunt Celia had spent the afternoon lying in a darkened guest room. Her husband remained at her side, solicitously dabbing at her temples with eau de cologne, and soothing her when she became agitated. Evidently before losing consciousness she had caught sight of one of the dead fish, and it was haunting her.

'Oh, it was horrible, loathsome!' she shuddered. 'I saw its vast white underbelly, bloated and mottled in the corruption of death! Oh, it was horrible!'

'Hush, my dearest,' Uncle Parker told her. 'It was a sight that was never meant for eyes so sensitive as yours. It *was* horrible, and I shall kill whoever was responsible.'

This made two people now out for Daisy's blood.

Aunt Celia was against Uncle Parker's killing the killer of the fish even before she knew that person to be her own daughter.

'Do not shed blood!' she pleaded. 'A rebuke will serve!'

Mr Bagthorpe had by now given up the idea of strangling Daisy. He had worked out the probable cost of draining and restocking the pond, doubled it, and come up with a hefty figure to add to the cost of the stags' heads. On top of this there was the notional figure of Mr Bagthorpe's loss of earnings as a result of being unable to Watch Goldfish. The sum he eventually came up with would, Uncle Parker later told him, have been ample to compensate George Bernard Shaw for his entire *oeuvre* going up in flames.

Most people were coming down to tea prepared for battle. Even Jack and William were at the ready.

'We're definitely being victimized,' William told Jack. 'Tess and Rosie haven't done a thing all day except blow and hack away on their instruments. Whatever I say, you back me up.'

'All right,' Jack agreed.

He quite liked doing things about the house for his mother. In his own mind, he counted this as a sort of honorary String to his Bow. The only other String he had was training Zero, and none of the rest of the family would allow even that.

'If ever that mutton-headed, pudding-footed hound learns to fetch a stick, it would not be a String to a Bow,' Mr Bagthorpe would say. 'It would be a miracle. I would notify the Pope.'

Grandma and Daisy appeared, Billy Goat Gruff in tow.

'Mummy Mummy Daddy Daddy!' Daisy squealed. 'Jus' guess what I got – I got some more friends! I got four Grandpa Gruffs and a Hobble-Gobble!'

'Darling,' murmured Aunt Celia fondly.

'Which being translated means four antique stags' heads of great value,' supplied Mr Bagthorpe, 'and an evil-smelling brute of a tramp who has downed a whole case of my malt Scotch.'

At this moment the evil-smelling brute of a tramp appeared. He brought with him a waft of expensive bath oil. Taller even than Uncle Parker, and with his long hair and beard and the purple robe draped about him, he was an imposing figure. He was barefoot, and this added to the impression of being a sage, a guru.

Everyone stared. The silence was broken by Daisy.

'It's my Hobble-Gobble! Oooh – and he got anunner frock!'

8

The tea party that followed was memorable even by Bagthorpian standards. At any given time as many as five different rows were going on. These were complicated by the fact that some people (notably Mr Bagthorpe) were involved in more than one argument, and had to keep flicking from one to another with the expertise of a Prosecution Counsel (or, in some cases, Counsel for the Defence).

The matter of the poisoned goldfish came up early on, and the younger Bagthorpes were in favour of downing tools and rushing out to inspect this sight, which was graphically described by their father. This triggered off Aunt Celia's memories.

'Oh . . . oh . . .' She pushed away her plate of lettuce. 'That loathsome, vast white underbelly, bloated and mottled . . .'

'Exactly,' said Mr Bagthorpe. 'You've hit the nail on the head for once, Celia.'

'I would rather you did not mention the fish in front of my wife, Henry,' said Uncle Parker dangerously.

'Me?' said Mr Bagthorpe. 'It's her that's burbling

on about vast white underbellies and blotches. And who *did* it? Who poured gallons of curdled milk into my two-thousand-quid pond?'

'Me! I did!' squealed Daisy triumphantly. There was not the least hint of remorse on her chubby face. 'Cos it's good for you, milk's good for you, in't it, Mummy?'

'Of course it is, my darling,' Aunt Celia confirmed.

'An' the poor lickle fish an't *got* no milk,' went on Daisy, 'and Mrs Fozzy got millions of milk. So I fetched it an' fetched it an' fetched it till I couldn't fetch no more 'cos I was tired!'

'It was an errand of mercy!' cried Aunt Celia.

'Mercy nothing!' snapped her brother. 'That brat of yours has put paid to every fish in that pond – you saw them, you saw them yourself! They must have died in agony – *you* saw their yellow sickly underbellies and bloated—'

'Steady, Henry,' warned Uncle Parker, as his wife began to moan and sway again. 'Celia has already had a severe trauma for one in her condition.'

'What condition?' demanded Mr Bagthorpe. 'She's always in that condition. Has been from childhood. Ask Mother.'

'I mean, Henry,' said Uncle Parker – he paused and lowered his voice – 'Her interesting condition.'

'It might interest you,' returned Mr Bagthorpe, the implication of this statement bypassing him completely. 'You're stuck with her. It doesn't interest me.

It's the state of my goldfish I'm interested in. And what compensation—'

'Henry!' his wife now interrupted him. She was gazing at Aunt Celia in disbelief and wonder. 'I think Russell is trying to tell us something very important. Are you, Russell?'

Uncle Parker looked inquiringly at his wife.

'Shall I?'

'I had hoped to keep it as a precious secret,' she murmured. 'A precious secret between ourselves and Daisy.'

'Oh, *dat* secret!' Her offspring nodded her golden ringlets. 'Der's going to be a lickle stranger,' she confided to the table at large. 'I been looking and looking, but I an't seen no lickle stranger.'

Comprehension was beginning to dawn.

'Celia!' Mrs Bagthorpe rose from her place and hastened down the table. 'Oh, Celia, darling! A baby!'

She made an ineffectual attempt at an embrace, while her spouse looked on with undisguised disbelief and horror.

'Ye gods!' he exclaimed. 'Do you *never* learn from experience, Russell?'

'There could never be another Daisy,' pronounced Grandma deflatingly.

Most present were inclined to agree with this.

'And a good job, too!' Mrs Fosdyke was heard to mutter.

'And what a blessing for mankind,' Mr O'Toole said warmly, 'that so fair a lady should people the earth!'

This had a distinctly gnomic ring, and evidently Aunt Celia thought so, because she rewarded him with a winning smile of the kind that made most men buckle at the knees. She was certainly very beautiful, though the Bagthorpes tended to take this for granted, in the same way they took for granted that they visited the dentist twice yearly.

'The archetypal Old Man,' Aunt Celia murmured. 'The fount of wisdom . . .'

She actually stretched a slender hand across the table towards him, and Mr O'Toole leaned forward, took it and kissed it, thereby arousing extreme jealously in Mrs Fosdyke's breast. She certainly could not compete with Aunt Celia in the looks stakes.

'Will you 'ave another stuffed egg, Mr O'Toole?' she inquired, stretching past his left ear to remove the plate from Grandpa, who was steadily emptying it.

The younger Bagthorpes were left more or less cold by the news that they were to have another cousin, with the exception of Rosie, who quite looked forward to there being someone she could read stories to, and whose hair she could plait as she sometimes did Daisy's. Even if it were a boy, she reflected, Aunt Celia would most likely let his hair grow long enough to plait.

'Once this child is born, you must consider your family complete, Aunt Celia,' Tess told her. 'For the sake of the environment.'

'Amen to that,' said Mr Bagthorpe. 'The damage done to the environment by the one you've already got is inestimable. It must resemble the National Debt.'

'The whole delicate balance of the universe is being threatened by overpopulation,' Tess continued. 'No family should have more than two children.'

Here she glanced reproachfully at her own parents.

'But that means Jack and me wouldn't be here!' objected Rosie.

'Exactly,' said William. 'Anonymous of Grimsby says the airways and airwaves are becoming congested. He says it's getting harder and harder to tune in to the Alien Intelligence in Outer Space.'

'I don't see what that's got to do with us,' said Jack, who was not going to agree that it would be better if he did not exist, despite his earlier promise.

'Anyway, I think your news is splendid, Celia and Russell,' said Mrs Bagthorpe, who was very keen on Family Feeling, and would herself have gone on to have several more children had not her husband refused to co-operate.

'I shall knit something, Celia,' Grandma promised. 'Probably in black.'

This offer was followed by a silence while everyone pondered this. It sounded more like a threat than a promise. Even Jack, who as a rule never noticed or thought about babies, felt sure he had never seen one in black.

'When I've finished me cardy, I'll do something,' offered Mrs Fosdyke.

This, given her opinion of Daisy seemed incon-
sistent. The truth was that Mrs Fosdyke doted on
babies, even Aunt Celia's. She had doted on Daisy
while she was still in her pram (which was not for
long. She had walked at nine months and started her
long career of mayhem and destruction by toppling
a Ming vase with a well-aimed teddy bear).

'What are you hoping for, Celia dear?' asked Mrs
Bagthorpe. 'A boy or a girl?'

'Oh, a girl, definitely.' Uncle Parker answered for
his wife. 'Celia feels that she would not know what
to say to a boy.'

'That figures,' said Mr Bagthorpe. 'I don't see Celia
standing yelling on the touchline or washing football
kit. Ha!'

'There is no reason why she should, Henry,' his
wife told him. Then, seeing the glimmer of an
opening to broach the topic of sexism, 'Russell could
quite easily do those things.'

'Russell?' echoed Mr Bagthorpe in disbelief. 'His
idea of sport is stretching out his arm for another gin
and tonic.'

'Exactly the same as your own, Henry,' agreed
Uncle Parker pleasantly. 'Except in your case, sub-
stitute Scotch for g and t.'

'You've never once come to watch me winning
cups at tennis, Father,' William told him.

'Or me winning black belts at judo,' added Tess
jealously.

'*Or* me swimming,' said Rosie. 'Other people's

fathers do. Charlotte Williams's father gets up and drives her to the swimming baths every morning at six o'clock.'

'Then more fool him,' said Mr Bagthorpe unrepentantly.

'The point I was making,' said Mrs Bagthorpe, who could not seem to steer the conversation at all, 'is that in these modern times both sexes must accept an equal share of responsibility in the home and the bringing up of children.'

'Don't be silly, Laura,' her husband told her. 'Save all that crap for that half-baked column of yours.'

'You are evading the issue, Father,' Tess told him coldly. 'What Mother is saying is perfectly true. Katie Reynolds's father does all the housework, and all the cooking and shopping and washing and ironing.'

'While her mother lies in bed writing a half-baked Problem page, I suppose,' said Mr Bagthorpe.

'Her mother is a brain surgeon.' Tess had hoped he would fall into this trap.

'Which, like writing a Problem Page, is at least of service to humanity.' Mrs Bagthorpe was encouraged by the way things were now going.

'Some of my friends think writing scripts isn't even a proper job at all,' piped up Rosie. 'Their fathers all do proper jobs like window cleaners and bank managers.'

Mr Bagthorpe was beginning to feel cornered.

'*And* their fathers don't go locking themselves in

their studies the minute anything needs doing,' Rosie went on.

'Henry has always been work shy,' Grandma said. 'And it has always been a sorrow to me that he did not enter an honourable profession. He simply did not have the application.'

'And what about him?' blustered Mr Bagthorpe, meaning Uncle Parker. 'What does that gin-swigging tailor's dummy ever do?'

'He is not my son,' replied Grandma. 'He is another woman's sorrow.'

The only time any of the Bagthorpes had seen Uncle Parker's mother was at his wedding. Looking like a slightly *passée Vogue* model she had swanned in and out of their lives. Nobody remembered much about her except Mr Bagthorpe, who claimed that she had drunk too much champagne. This was understandable, he said, at the time, having finally got Uncle Parker off her hands. He now pretended to believe that she was a dipsomaniac, and that Uncle Parker had her hidden away somewhere.

'Like that lunatic in *Jane Eyre*,' he said, 'or Rumpelstiltskin.'

As usual, his literary references were hopelessly adrift. He had meant Rapunzel, and there was no suggestion that even she was mad, or drank.

'I shall 'ave to be off now,' announced Mrs Fosdyke, who intended to let the Bagthorpes sort out among themselves who should perform the various chores that did not qualify as Occasional Thurpy.

'Thank you so much for your delicious meal,' Mrs Bagthorpe said. 'Don't forget your knitting in the fridge.'

'Knitting in the *where*?' asked Mr Bagthorpe as she left.

'Refrigerator, Henry,' his wife replied. 'She puts it in there to keep cool in hot weather. It is a very sensible idea. If you ever did any knitting yourself you would know how sticky the pins can become.'

'I shall put *my* knitting in the refrigerator, too,' Grandma announced.

She did, too. So did Mrs Bagthorpe, once the Big Knit for Aunt Celia's baby got under way. In weeks to come it became increasingly difficult to find the margarine, or the yoghurt in among a mounting tangle of wool and pins.

'Mrs Fosdyke is more inspired in her thinking than any other member of this household,' Grandma continued, sensing that things were going off the boil.

'The woman's an imbecile,' said her son, rising to the bait. 'She'll be putting those fur-edged slippers of hers in the oven to warm next.'

'Perhaps it is the soothing action of pushing the Hoover to and fro, or dusting, that induces a meditative state.' Mrs Bagthorpe was beavering away like anything at her theme. 'Perhaps you should try it, Henry.'

Her husband would never, ever, have put the words 'soothing' and 'Hoover' in the same sentence.

'If I wish to induce a meditative state I Watch

Goldfish,' he told her. 'Or rather, I used to. I doubt whether watching that lot floating about with their vast white greenish yellow bloated underbellies . . .'

Aunt Celia had her hands over her ears.

'I think perhaps I had better take Celia home,' said Uncle Parker.

'Why don't you?' said Mr Bagthorpe. 'And don't forget that stinking goat and brat while you're about it.'

'And my Grandpa Gruffs,' piped up Daisy. 'Mummy, Daddy, I got four Grandpa Gruffs! Come and look!'

She tugged at Aunt Celia's flowing sleeve with one hand and reached for Billy Goat Gruff's ribbons with the other. Unprotestingly, Aunt Celia allowed herself to be led into the hall, followed by Uncle Parker and Mr Bagthorpe.

'They're valuable objects,' he told the Parkers as they stood staring at the stags' heads. 'All the more so because they're motheaten. It's proof of their authenticity.'

'I would hardly imagine anyone would wish to fake such objects,' murmured Uncle Parker.

'You'd be surprised,' said Mr Bagthorpe. 'There's a big international market in stags' heads. In America, you haven't arrived till you've got one. They're faked by the thousand, and smuggled in through Morocco.'

He was, as usual, overdoing it, as well as betraying his hopeless grasp of geography.

'What about camels' heads?' mused Uncle Parker. 'Any market in those?'

'Mummy, Daddy, I want them!' Daisy now inter-rupted. 'I got one Grandpa, and now Billy Goat Gruff's got four!'

'Of course, darling,' her mother told her. 'What an unselfish thought!'

'At least this lot won't make puddles, Russell,' Mr Bagthorpe told Uncle Parker. 'Five hundred.'

'You are, of course, joking.'

'Seven hundred to anyone else,' Mr Bagthorpe said. 'It's as well to keep these heirlooms in the family.'

'Their eyes, so deep, so timid and mild . . .' said Aunt Celia dreamily, unwittingly batting for her brother. 'One could almost drown in their liquid depths . . .'

It sounded rather as though she intended to take up Stags' Head Gazing instead of Goldfish and Fountain Watching. Uncle Parker himself evidently thought so, because he fished out his cheque book without further demur.

Mr Bagthorpe should have been delighted by this five hundred per cent profit on what had been, after all, purely accidental purchases. But his enjoyment was spoiled by the careless way his brother-in-law proposed to pay such an exorbitant sum for four of the scabbiest stags' heads Mr Bagthorpe had himself ever seen, even in use as hat racks in nightclubs. It strengthened Mr Bagthorpe's jealous suspicion that Uncle Parker had money to burn (which, given Daisy's propensity for starting fires, was just as well). Nobody had ever seen Uncle Parker do a day's work. He did not even cultivate his garden. He employed a gardener, and would sit for hours sipping gin and tonic, watching him at work. He found it soothing, he said.

'Don't bother filling that cheque in,' Mr Bagthorpe now told him. 'You're not through yet. There's my pond and fish.'

He was too late. Uncle Parker tore off the cheque and handed it to him.

'Some other time,' he said. 'If people leave hundreds of milk bottles in the vicinity of a creative four-year-old, they must be held in some way responsible for the consequences. I'll have a word with my lawyers.'

He picked up a couple of the stags' heads and moved off, clearly expecting his wife and daughter to follow. Daisy, however, was not yet satisfied. She had her Grandpa Gruffs, now she wanted her Hobble-Gobble. Again she tugged at her mother's sleeve.

'Mummy, Mummy, I want der Hobble-Gobble!'

'Hear that, Russell?' cried Mr Bagthorpe, delighted. 'Got a few cases of gin in, have you?'

'There's no room in the car, Daisy,' her father told her. 'We'll come back for him tomorrow.'

He intended no such thing, and Mr Bagthorpe knew it.

'Laura'll drive him over for you,' he offered. 'She might even have another spare frock for him. Ha!'

'The sage, the Ancient, the Wise Man . . .' Aunt

Celia was off on her own again. 'Daisy has discovered her own guru . . .'

'Too right, Celia,' Mr Bagthorpe agreed, hugely enjoying his brother-in-law's discomfiture. 'If you let him slip through your fingers now, she may never find another. I tell you what, Russell, leave the stags' heads and take the guru. You can nip back for them later.'

Unfortunately for him Grandma had overheard this exchange.

'I never heard such ill-bred nonsense, Henry,' she told her son. 'Mr O'Toole is an old friend of Alfred's, and our house guest. You cannot simply pass him over like a stag's head. Where are your manners?'

Mr Bagthorpe had never pretended to have any manners, nor did he now.

'Bilge, Mother,' he returned. 'Hogwash. He's a stinking, evil Salvation Army reject who swigged all my Scotch. Best malt.'

'Besides which, you will doubtless be glad of his assistance in the housework, Henry,' she continued.

He stared.

'In the what? You're rambling, Mother.'

'From now on all the household duties will be performed by the male sex,' she told him, having evidently grasped this much of her earlier indoctrination by Tess and Rosie. 'We shall then be liberated.'

Mrs Bagthorpe joined the group in the hall just in time to hear this last declaration.

'Liberated!' she cried in ringing tones. Hearing this

clarion call her daughters ran out from the dining room and ranged themselves beside her.

'From now on there will be an equitable apportionment of duties,' said Tess.

'We're on strike,' added Rosie.

'You're mad,' Mr Bagthorpe told them. 'We've already got that woman everlastingly hedgehogging about with brooms and Hoovers.'

'She's on strike as well,' Rosie informed him.

'If you are referring to Mrs Fosdyke,' Mrs Bagthorpe said, 'you are mistaken, Henry. She has returned, but only to carry out culinary duties. It is on the advice of her doctor.'

'The man's a fool,' he replied. 'We all know it. He doesn't know leprosy from housemaid's knee.'

'Perhaps you may soon find yourself in a position to confirm that,' Grandma told him. 'Unused as you are to kneeling and scrubbing floors.'

Jack and William now appeared.

'You've been picking on Jack and me all day, Mother,' said William. 'Jack and me are fed up. It's all your fault, Father – just because you go locking yourself up in your study every time there's any work to do—'

'You do, you do!' cried Rosie passionately, quite forgetting that she was supposed to be in the opposite camp to her brothers.

Mr Bagthorpe looked wildly about him. The Parkers, and his chance of off-loading the bibulous Mr O'Toole, had slipped through his fingers. He could hear the spurt of gravel as Uncle Parker accelerated off. He glared back at his glaring family. In the end all he could come up with was a well-worn threat.

'I may have to go and stay with Great-Aunt Lucy in Torquay,' he told them. He nipped nimbly past them into the study, and shut the door.

9

When Mr O'Toole strolled down to the Fiddler's Arms that evening it was not to keep a secret assignation with Mrs Fosdyke. It was, quite simply, in search of a drink. The bottle of brandy kept for cooking had evidently been put back wherever Mrs Fosdyke hid it, and the chances of his being offered a drink by Mr Bagthorpe were, he correctly surmised, nil.

His clothes were still in the washing machine, but he was not in the least self-conscious about wandering down the leafy lanes to the village in Mrs Bagthorpe's sari. He had never much worried about appearances, and assumed that no one else did. He was mildly surprised by the number of cars whose drivers, on catching sight of the huge, bearded figure swathed in purple, braked and swerved violently, but did not connect this phenomenon with himself. He was no longer barefoot, but wore a pair of woven Afghan slipper socks which were much easier on his bunions than his old boots. In his pocket was a five-pound note loaned to him by Grandma. He hummed in little snatches as he went.

Nothing in their previous experience had prepared the regulars of the Fiddler's Arms for the apparition that now entered. Voices stopped in mid-sentence, darts froze in flight. There was silence save for the sound of several clients choking on their beer. To all appearances the Emperor of Siam had just walked in.

Mr O'Toole padded majestically to the bar and the locals fell back to give him way.

''Tis a pleasant evening,' he observed. No one contradicted.

'It's 'im!' Mrs Fosdyke whispered hoarsely. Her cronies peered and craned, neither of them having seen a millionaire, eccentric or otherwise, in the flesh.

'Oooh, you can tell 'e's somebody, just to look at 'im!' whispered Mrs Pye.

'That's a frock of Mrs Bagthorpe's 'e's got on,' Mrs Fosdyke hissed. 'Suits 'im, don't it?'

Mesdames Pye and Bates were by no means enlightened souls. Their minds were narrow, and ran on tracks laid down in the far distant past. They were loud in their condemnation of long hair, shaved heads, punk hair, earrings on men, earrings through noses (of either sex). They were also vocal on the subjects of black leather and studs, hippie convoys and Chinese takeaways, which usually, Mrs Bates maintained, contained cat and dog meat and also, she would not be surprised, marijuana concealed in the beansprouts (which she would not touch with a barge pole, let alone a chopstick, anyhow).

'They mix it in to get you under their influence,' she said darkly. 'That's what marryana does. Then you're 'ooked, you 'ave to go back again and again.'

When Mrs Fosdyke and Mrs Pye challenged this last claim she asked them why, in that case, the Potters next door but one were down there at the Chinese every night fetching carrier bags of the stuff home? Neither lady could imagine, and said so shudderingly, and the point was conceded.

Neither Mrs Pye nor Mrs Bates had ever seen a man in a frock before, except on television, and had certainly never thought to live to see one mingling with the regulars in their favourite haunt. Had they not been in possession of the knowledge that this person was a multimillionaire they would have had a great deal to say about it. As it was, visions of whole bundles of ten-pound notes being carelessly distributed quite reconciled them to the bizarre appearance of Mr O'Toole. Indeed, they were lavish in their praise.

''E's a fine figure of a man,' said Mrs Bates.

'Oh, 'e is,' affirmed Mrs Fosdyke smugly, as if she were herself responsible for this. ''E's bigger than any of them, even that Mr Parker.'

'I like a beard on a man,' Mrs Pye confided. 'It distinguishes 'em. Ever so many kings of England had beards, you know.'

'Are there any pockets in that frock?' inquired Mrs Bates obscurely. (She was speculating as to the possibility of bundles of tenners being secreted about his person.)

'Shall I ask 'im over?' asked Mrs Fosdyke recklessly, enchanted by her friends' reactions to her protégé.

'Ooooh, yes, go on, Glad!' urged Mrs Pye.

'I should think 'e's ever so interesting to talk to,' said Mrs Bates.

Thus encouraged Mrs Fosdyke, quite pink and girlish, half-rose in her seat and uttered a piercing, 'Cooee!', waving her handbag as she did so.

Mr O'Toole, having just downed his first double Scotch under the concerted eyes of the regulars, turned.

'By all the saints!' he exclaimed. 'If it isn't herself!'

All eyes now turned to see whom he could possibly mean. He shambled towards the trio in the corner.

'If it isn't herself whose every mouthful is a foretaste of heaven!'

His audience, taking 'mouthful' to refer to Mrs Fosdyke's utterances rather than her cooking, thought this was going it a bit. Some of them, having been on the receiving end of her mouthfuls in the past, began to think that the stranger in their midst was even madder than he looked. They quickly swallowed their beer and left.

Mr O'Toole, having reached the table in the corner, and seeing one of Mrs Fosdyke's hands lying spare on it, seized it and pressed it to his lips. He had never done much of this at the Salvation Army, but found that it seemed to go down very well with the Bagthorpes – as it did now.

Mrs Fosdyke simpered and cast triumphant looks

at her cronies, who were now reduced to nervous giggles at the close proximity of this massive multimil–lionaire. They had no idea of how they should behave in this novel social situation. Each secretly toyed with the idea of rising and curtseying, each wished fervently she had worn her best hat, and had her hair permed more recently.

Mr O'Toole, intuiting that Mrs Fosdyke would not wish him to devalue her own tribute by bestowing it on her companions, contented himself with making a half-bow to each in turn. The saloon bar, still engulfed in eerie silence, watched fascinated. Hand-kissing and bows were very thin on the ground as a rule in the Fiddler's Arms. There, back slaps and even punches were more the order of the day.

'Fancy you coming down 'ere honouring us, Mr O'Toole!' gushed Mrs Fosdyke. 'Meet my friends. This is Mrs Pye, and that's Mrs Bates. Ever such old friends we are. Known each other since we was at school.'

'Charmed,' said Mr O'Toole. 'And what will ye lovely ladies be drinking?'

They told him. He returned to the bar and ordered two port and lemons, a Guinness and a double Scotch. These were duly produced by the dazed landlord. Mr O'Toole proffered the change from his original five-pound note.

'I shall want another one pound eighty-three, sir,' the landlord told him nervously.

The ladies in the corner watched keenly to see

from whence he would produce the bundles of tenners.

Mr O'Toole threw up his hands in horror.

'Oh – if I'm not altogether forgetting I'm not in my trousers!'

The situation was entirely new in the landlord's experience. He dimly comprehended that what the stranger was saying was that his money was in his trousers – wherever they might be. He was saying that he had not the money to pay for the drinks he had just ordered. He was evidently so shocked by the oversight of his trousers, that he reached for the Scotch and downed it at a gulp.

The landlord looked helplessly about and was met by the inscrutable faces of the saloon bar regulars. They were waiting to see what he would do. Should he refuse to hand over the remaining drinks, call the police, or pass the whole thing off by saying, 'Never mind, sir – some other time will do,' and put it down to experience? He would put a sign on the door in future, saying 'No drinks served to persons of the male sex in frocks.'

Meanwhile the ladies in the corner were agog.

''E's like royalty, see!' hissed Mrs Fosdyke. ''E don't carry money. It's beneath 'im.'

'You can't expect Sam to know that,' said Mrs Pye. ''Ow's 'e to know 'e's a millionaire?'

This was a fair question. There was not the least clue in Mr O'Toole's appearance to suggest that he was a secret millionaire.

Mrs Fosdyke acted. She left her seat and scuttled over to the bar, where she rummaged in her handbag for her purse.

'How much was it you said, Sam?' she inquired casually.

'Oh – Glad – one eighty-three, please,' replied the landlord thankfully.

'Oh, the shame of it!' cried Mr O'Toole. 'To treat a lady, and her to pay! Another double, please, landlord!'

By the time Mrs Fosdyke had found her purse she was another two pounds down. She cared not a fig. This was her hour of glory. She was standing drinks to a multimillionaire.

'Mr O'Toole's stopping with the Bagthorpes, you know,' she informed the landlord.

This, so far as he was concerned, explained a good deal. The inmates of Unicorn House were generally believed to be lunatics – largely on the testimony of Mrs Fosdyke herself, who did not know the meaning of the word loyalty. (Neither, to be fair, did the Bagthorpes.)

Mrs Fosdyke toyed with the idea of confiding in Sam that Mr O'Toole was a disguised millionaire. She wisely decided against this. If she told him, she was telling the whole village. Once Mr O'Toole's cover was blown he would almost certainly depart, to scatter his bundles of tenners elsewhere. She made a mental note to swear her friends to secrecy.

Those ladies were charmed by the company of Mr

O'Toole, who before long was begging them to call him Joseph – or even Irish Joe, which was, he said, the name by which he was known the length and breadth of England. They coyly brought themselves to address him as Joseph, but could never, as they afterwards told one another, have brought themselves to call him Irish Joe.

'Makes him sound like a tramp, or something!' Mrs Bates said, and her friends heartily agreed.

Mr O'Toole did not leave the Fiddler's Arms until closing time, by which time Mrs Fosdyke's purse was empty, but her cup correspondingly flowing over. They left together, her arm tucked in his and her head filled with bundles of tenners high as haystacks.

Meanwhile, back at Unicorn House, things had not stood still. With the Bagthorpes they never did. Their lives had a built-in momentum of their own. One event led inexorably to another in a rapidly and fatally descending spiral.

Not long after Uncle Parker had left he had returned. Mr Bagthorpe, forewarned by the spurt of gravel, instantly guessed the reason for the visit. He darted out of his study, picked up the two remaining stags' heads and ran with them into the kitchen. Seeing no convenient hiding place, he opened the pantry door and tossed the heads inside. He slammed the door, raced back to the hall and was there, albeit somewhat out of breath, when Uncle Parker pushed at the half-open door and entered.

'What're you doing back here?' demanded Mr

Bagthorpe. 'Should you not be back at your place, ungumming your fountain?'

Uncle Parker glanced about him.

'Just popped back for the other two heads,' he said. 'Daisy is unable to sleep without them, she says.'

'She is never taking them to bed with her?' Mr Bagthorpe was incredulous.

'I fear so,' sighed Uncle Parker.

'Then it's to be hoped she's impaled on their horns in the night,' said Mr Bagthorpe heartlessly. He had no way of reading from his brother-in-law's expression whether or not he agreed. Uncle Parker had a very strong line in sang-froid.

'I – er – don't seem to see them,' he said.

'Nor will you,' returned Mr Bagthorpe. 'I'm keeping them as surety.'

'For what, exactly?' queried Uncle Parker.

'You know perfectly well for what,' replied Mr Bagthorpe. 'When you settle the bill for my three-thousand-pound pond, then you can have 'em.'

'I told you, Henry. I shall have to consult my lawyers.'

'You consult 'em,' Mr Bagthorpe replied. 'Bring 'em to look. Let *them* see the vast white blotched greenish yellow bloated underbellies of—'

He broke off, remembering that Celia was not present to be affected.

'The state of the fish is not in question,' Uncle Parker told him. 'It is the liability that has to be determined.'

'Liability?' echoed Mr Bagthorpe. 'If that unhinged, benighted, unholy brat—'

'She's not, she's not!'

At this point Rosie, who had eavesdropped on the previous exchange, poked her head over the banisters.

'Daisy's sweet!' she screamed. 'And it's sweet to take the stags' heads to bed with her! I'm going to ask if I can take a photo of it!'

'You do that,' her father told her. 'It is the only way anyone else would ever believe it.'

'And you give Uncle Parker the other two stags' heads this very minute! Else Daisy'll never get to sleep!'

'Then she must stay awake,' said Mr Bagthorpe. 'You can stop up all night and play chess with her, Russell. It'll bring your game on no end. Ha!'

Grandma, having heard the name of her favourite, now emerged from her room where she had retired disconsolate when Daisy had departed. The absence of Daisy always left a big hole in her existence (and, indeed, that of anyone who knew her, though for different reasons).

'What is the matter?' she inquired. 'Is Daisy being persecuted yet again?'

'Yes, she is!' cried Rosie. 'Father won't let her have her Grandpa Gruffs, and she wants to take them to bed with her!'

'Such heartlessness does not surprise me,' Grandma said. 'Henry has never had any rapport with the minds of innocent children.'

'I've never met any!' Mr Bagthorpe snapped. 'And so far as I'm concerned, this conversation is now over!'

He could take on Uncle Parker and Grandma singly, but now that they seemed likely to join forces he beat a strategic withdrawal. He went into the study and banged the door, which gave him the satisfying feeling of having retired the victor.

'Tell you what . . .' said Uncle Parker, eyeing Rosie thoughtfully. 'That was a first-class idea of yours, about those photos.'

'Oh – can I come and take them now, can I?'

'And why not stop the night, while you're about it?'

Uncle Parker had all too clearly seen the possibility of Daisy's staying awake all night. Whether or not he had to do so himself, the prospect of a frustrated Daisy roaming The Knoll during the small hours was a daunting one. It could be razed to the ground by morning, he thought.

'Oh, Uncle Parker, thank you!' Rosie rushed to hug him. 'I wish you were my father!'

Mr Bagthorpe, with his ear to the study door, heard this treachery and ground his teeth.

'Perhaps I could come myself?' said Grandma jealously. Seeing her son-in-law look dubious, she added, 'I think that a mother needs to be at her daughter's side at a time like this. Celia is clearly in need of wise counsel.'

Here she touched a raw nerve, and knew it.

'Of course!' Uncle Parker exclaimed. 'Go and pack your overnight bags, the pair of you!'

Hugely delighted by this unexpected development, Grandma and Rosie set off upstairs to pack.

'Though bear in mind that my car is not a station wagon!' he called after them. He knew Grandma's propensity to dismantle and remove her whole room when she went away. 'Or, indeed, a furniture van!' he added *sotto voce*, for the benefit of Mr Bagthorpe.

Mrs Bagthorpe now came hurrying down.

'Ah, Russell! Rosie tells me that you have invited herself and Mother to stay the night. How very kind!'

'Mother is coming to give Celia wise counsel,' he told her, 'and Rosie is coming to keep Daisy company. Henry refuses to part with that other pair of stags' heads I just paid an exorbitant price for.'

'Henry is most uncooperative,' she said. 'I expect he has shut himself in his study again?'

'Just so,' he replied.

'That is his immediate reaction to anything that does not suit him. One wonders whether he should perhaps see a psychiatrist. He seems quite unable to face up to reality.'

Both were well aware that Mr Bagthorpe had his ear to the study door.

'I, of course, have been advising a psychiatrist for years,' said Uncle Parker. 'But one wonders if he is not now too far gone.'

Rosie joined them, carrying Little Tommy in his basket.

'I'm afraid he's got to come as well,' she told Uncle Parker.

'He will be company for Billy Goat Gruff,' said Mrs Bagthorpe sensibly.

It was indeed true that Little Tommy and the goat seemed to have a certain rapport. They played noisy games of tag and hide and seek, though they had not yet done so at The Knoll. It was now Aunt Celia's turn, Mrs Bagthorpe reflected uncharitably, to have her ornaments knocked over and curtains brought down.

'Grandma's not quite ready yet,' said Rosie. 'But I've talked her out of bringing her photos and things.'

'Good girl. Tell you what, got your camera?'

She nodded.

'Just nip out into the drive, will you, and photograph that line of milk bottles.'

Rosie looked askance.

'Take shots from various angles. It will be a novel composition, Rosie. Might even win a prize with it.'

She brightened, nodded, and went off with her camera.

'Mind you get 'em all in!' he cried after her.

What was really in his mind was that Mr Bagthorpe might start tampering with the evidence. He was quite capable of carting the bottles down to the pool and tipping them in, claiming this to be Daisy's work. In his study, Mr Bagthorpe, who had indeed had this in mind, gnawed on his knuckles.

Tess now appeared and demanded to know what was going on.

'Is it true you're letting Rosie and Grandma skive off to The Knoll, Mother? What about the Rota?'

Tess herself had no desire to go and stay with the Parkers, but suspected her sister's motive in doing so.

'I am still in the process of drawing it up, Tess,' her mother told her. 'I am also formulating some House Rules.'

The sudden cessation of drumming overhead indicated William's imminent arrival on the scene. His reaction on learning of Rosie and Grandma's departure was much the same as his sister's.

'I shan't do Rosie's stint while she's gone,' he informed his mother. 'I am composing a solo symphony for drums.'

'What an original idea, William!' cried Mrs Bagthorpe. 'Will it create a precedent?'

'I should think so,' he told her laconically.

'Fortunately,' added Tess, 'I myself can undertake only light duties. I intend to translate the entire dramatic works of Molière.'

'Do you really?' said Mrs bagthorpe dubiously. 'Is that really necessary, Tess?'

'Scholarship and necessity are strangers to one another,' Tess informed her loftily. 'Where's Jack?'

No one knew. He was in fact down by the pool, trying to resuscitate goldfish.

'There's only you and me in this family really care

about dumb animals,' he told Zero, who lay near by toying with a stick.

He combed the pool with a rake, thereby breaking up the curdles and destroying evidence. Each time he dredged up a goldfish he raked it in and dropped it into a bucket of water. He did not quite know what he expected this to achieve, but definitely felt he was doing the goldfish a good turn.

Soon there were half a dozen of them in the bucket. Jack peered hopefully down at them. They showed no sign of life. They were big fish, and very crowded in there. Moreover, they seemed to be floating with vast white bloated underbellies upward.

Jack had been learning mouth-to-mouth resuscitation at school but did not feel like trying this on the goldfish. The case looked hopeless. He did not, however, as a Bagthorpe, give up easily.

'What else . . . ?' he wondered. Then, 'Brandy!'

This was a much favoured restorative in the household. Jack, unlike his father and Mr O'Toole, did know where Mrs Fosdyke hid her bottle of cooking brandy.

He lifted the bucket and set off back to the house, taking care not to slop the goldfish out. Zero padded after him.

When Jack entered the pantry he was somewhat surprised to find that Mrs Fosdyke had put the stags' heads in there. Surely she could not be contemplating using them in a stew, or to make pâté? He wasted little time debating this. He took the bottle of brandy from its hiding place and poured a liberal dose into the bucket.

'I'll leave you in here overnight where it's cool and quiet,' he told his patients. 'Just keep saying to yourselves, "I will live, I will live!"'

Which was more or less what Mr Bagthorpe was saying to himself in his study, though without any real conviction.

10

The Knoll had always been something of a mystery to the Bagthorpes. Uncle Parker guarded his family's privacy, as Mr Bagthorpe was wont to say, as a Mafia boss guards his privacy. He had recently installed an electronic system to open the front gates only to selected callers. This had filled Mr Bagthorpe with bitter envy. His own methods of deterring unwanted callers were more primitive. He would hammer on the study window and grimace horribly, shaking a fist. Many a frightened flag-seller or collector of jumble had turned and fled at this apparition. On occasion Mr Bagthorpe would run out of the front door and after them, still yelling.

He would dearly have liked Uncle Parker's more sophisticated deterrent.

'That accursed woman would never again set foot in my house, for one!' he thought, meaning Mrs Fosdyke. He could also refuse entry to the Parkers and their goat. He could even lock Grandma out, if he got the chance.

The truth was, of course, that all these people were life's blood to Mr Bagthorpe. Without the stimulus of their presence he would have gone into a galloping decline. He was addicted to his own adrenalin.

The main reason why Uncle Parker did not invite the Bagthorpes to The Knoll was to protect his wife. Her sensitivity was such that she could take them only in very small doses. Also, she did not want the vibrations of her tranquil home polluted by those of the Bagthorpes, as Uncle Parker had once tactlessly explained.

'She needs peace as a rose needs dew,' he claimed.

'Rose my elbow!' Mr Bagthorpe had told him. 'Celia doesn't need any hostile vibrations from outside – she's got her own worm within the bud – ha!'

He meant, of course, Daisy. Over the years that infant had certainly, from all accounts, blazed a fearsome trail through her home, and this quite literally. At one time smoke had been seen rising above the trees surrounding The Knoll with a regularity that suggested there was an Indian encampment in there, or a kipper factory.

Daisy experimented with water, too, and wrote poems on the walls. There was also the goat.

The only time the Bagthorpes had ever been invited *en masse* to The Knoll was on the occasion of The Banquet. Even then none of them had penetrated much further than the dining room, which had itself been destroyed early on in the proceedings.

Rosie had occasionally visited Daisy, but her recollections of the house were hazy. She had been too busy, she said, to notice. In any case, as Mr Bagthorpe pointed out, the place had to be redecorated at such frequent intervals that it was probably never the same twice running.

The only other person who had visited was Grandma. She had taken her Fortnum and Mason hamper and her cat and stayed with the Parkers during her son's drive for Self-Sufficiency. She could easily have given a description of The Knoll, not a detail of which had escaped her keen eye, but refused to do so.

'It would be a betrayal of hospitality,' she declared. 'Dear Celia wishes to keep her home sacrosanct. It is her haven, her refuge from a cruel world.'

She sounded like Uncle Parker, rather.

Rosie and Grandma left for The Knoll waved off only by Mrs Bagthorpe who was very sentimental about leaving and homecomings. Whenever a member of the family went away, if only for an overnight camp, she would light what she called a 'homecoming candle' to celebrate the return. Everyone else thought this custom extremely soppy, and told her so. If Mr Bagthorpe ever went away, the first thing he would do on his return was to blow the welcome candle out, saying, 'That's put paid to that piffle!'

Both Rosie and Grandma were much looking forward to their stay. Both adored Daisy, and thought her perfect. The former, as well as photographing Daisy in bed snuggled up to her stags' heads, intended to take photographs of the interior of the house. She would then send them up to *Ideal Home*, which was looking for houses to feature. The latter intended to give her pregnant daughter as much wise counsel as she could fit in. This would consist mainly of urging her to eat plenty of red meat, and take a brisk five-mile walk each day.

Uncle Parker drove through his electronically operated gates and up the drive. Rosie was struck by the way he rolled the car gently over his own gravel. When he drove up to Unicorn House he left the gravel in deep furrows, like the wake of a ship. She supposed that he did not want to disturb his wife, who was probably meditating.

Aunt Celia went in a lot for meditating. Mr Bagthorpe, indeed, said that she spent her entire life in a trance.

'Awake – asleep – what's the difference?' he would say, not entirely without justification. She certainly did seem to drift in and out of consciousness and was probably suffering, as Mrs Fosdyke alleged, from an overdose of lettuce. Her daughter, however, more than made up for this. Daisy was always on the ball. She could survive on a minimum of sleep and was often at her most active during the small hours. Mr Bagthorpe said that she should be force fed with lettuce.

The house itself now came into view. It was at first not clearly recognizable as a house, covered as it was with rambling roses and creepers of all kinds.

'Celia thinks of it as her bower,' Uncle Parker would explain to bemused visitors, searching for the door.

'Daisy's already tucked up,' Uncle Parker now optimistically told his passengers as he drew up. 'Creep up and surprise her, why don't you?'

This idea appealed especially to Rosie, who wanted to catch Daisy and her stags' heads unaware, to get a spontaneous shot.

They tiptoed into the hall. This was panelled, with a wide oak staircase and minstrels' gallery. Here and there were suits of armour and medieval tapestries. It had been specially created to harmonize with Aunt Celia's mood whenever she was in one of her Guinevere phases. It was a wonder, Mr Bagthorpe said, that there wasn't a sword stuck in a stone.

Ancient oak staircases do not lend themselves to successful tiptoeing, and Rosie and Grandma creaked their way up. Rosie noticed that Daisy had crayoned one of her favourite poems on the panelling – AL THE BEEZ ARE DED. Higher up was a new one – MILIONS IS A BIZZY NUMBER LIK THE STARS. Higher up still was posed the bald question – WOT ABOUT ANTS AN THERE TEENY HEDS?

Rosie was stumped by this, and made a mental note to question Daisy about it later. She heard Grandma's ecstatic whisper, 'The mind of that child is fathomless!' and felt bound to agree.

Daisy's reception of her unexpected visitors was warm. When they edged open the door of her room they discovered her not in bed, as they had expected, but up and doing.

'Der, you darlin' ole Grandpa Gruff!' they heard her exclaim. 'Who's a pretty boy, den?'

Daisy was embellishing her new pets, evidently feeling that they had to keep their end up with Billy Goat Gruff, who was always elaborately turned out in satin ribbons and bells, trimmed like a Christmas tree. They saw that Daisy had already decorated one stag's head. Its horns were barely visible. One was stacked with bracelets, the other twined with beads.

'Titania and Bottom!' said Grandma fondly, and Daisy turned.

'Oooh, it's darlin' lickle Gramma Bag!' She abandoned her half-trimmed stag and rushed to embrace her. She hugged Rosie, too, but not with the same fervour. Grandma and she were kindred spirits, soul mates.

'We've come instead of the other two Grandpa Gruffs,' Rosie explained. 'Father's hidden them.'

'I wather have oo,' replied Daisy generously. Then, thoughtfully, 'You an't got no horns to decowate.'

'Where is your mother, Daisy?' Grandma asked. 'She should be eating plenty of red meat and taking five-mile walks.'

'Mummy don't eat no meat 'cos it's dead,' said Daisy. 'An she don't walk. She does stretchy dancing.'

This was true. Aunt Celia kept lithe and swaying by performing Isadora-Duncan-type dances, often barefoot and in the dew.

'Any case, she's finking booful,' added Daisy, matter-of-factly.

What this meant was that Aunt Celia had embarked on a policy of Thinking Beautiful Thoughts, for the benefit of her unborn child. She tended to do a lot of this anyway, so there was no marked difference in her behaviour. She said that every thought she had affected the baby, every sight she saw, every note of music she heard. It was lucky that she was not exposed to Grandma's cracked Valkyries. This would have boded ill for any unborn child.

While awaiting the birth of Daisy Aunt Celia had read Keats, Wordsworth and Yeats, and listened continuously to Bach and Mozart. She evidently thought that this had paid off handsomely, though few others could see it. Mr Bagthorpe said that she might just as well have read the Marquis de Sade and listened to aboriginal tribal chants, for all the difference it would have made.

'That child is sensitive like a Black Widow Spider is sensitive,' he would say.

Aunt Celia was indeed at that present moment deep into Thinking Beautiful. She was in her own room, which she called The Bower and had designed herself. It was like a cross between the tropical house at Kew and a pottery exhibition. There was a trickling fountain in there, which Uncle Parker had now ungummed, and hidden speakers relayed the strains of an Elgar symphony. Aunt Celia was reclining in a white hammock strung among the foliage, and was gazing at a reproduction of a Botticelli madonna. She herself might easily have posed as the model for this.

One would be tempted to think that Grandma had herself gazed at such paintings while awaiting the birth of her own daughter, had not such an activity been so totally out of character. It was easy to see how Grandma had produced Mr Bagthorpe, but a mystery how she had come up with Aunt Celia.

Having off-loaded Grandma and Rosie, Uncle Parker went straight along to The Bower to inform his wife of their arrival.

'Lovely, darling,' she murmured. She did not, as eager hostess, roll straight out of her hammock and busy herself with arrangements for their comfort. On the contrary, she closed her eyes.

'Will they stay long?' she inquired.

'Not on your life!' he replied. 'I'll get those stags' heads tomorrow, never you fear, one way or another. Probably enlist Jack. You stay there, beloved, Thinking Beautiful. I'll sort Rosie and Mother out.'

He planted a kiss on her smooth brow and went out, closing the door quietly behind him. He then went down to inspect the larder.

The Parkers never entertained house guests, as a rule. For one thing, they had few friends, being totally absorbed in one another (or rather, both totally absorbed in Aunt Celia). Even had this not been so, any friends would have quailed at the prospect of a diet of lettuce and wheatgerm, relieved occasionally by the odd bowl of clear soup, enlivened only by a few floating herbs. If invited for a weekend, they would surely have thought up cogent reasons to be elsewhere.

Uncle Parker was well aware that Rosie and Grandma would expect something more substantial than this. In any case, both he and his daughter were normal healthy eaters, though any partaking of red meat had to be done out of Aunt Celia's sight. (She had to be kept right away when sirloin, for instance, was being roasted. She said she could smell the blood.) Mrs Chivers, who came in, was a fair cook, though not in the same league as Mrs Fosdyke. Over the years Uncle Parker had himself become a passable cook, and could jug a mean hare.

In the kitchen he mopped up a couple of Billy Goat Gruff's puddles, humming under his breath. He then satisfied himself that there were the ingredients for breakfast. He and Daisy often began the day with a good fry-up. Aunt Celia never faced the world until eleven o'clock. Uncle Parker would take her lemon tea and freshly squeezed orange juice on a tray, and then she would go winding through her private rituals of meditation and stretchy dancing.

There were plenty of bacon, eggs, sausages and so forth.

'I'll whip 'em straight back to Unicorn House as soon as I've fed 'em,' he thought. He was well pleased with his strategy in bringing Grandma and Rosie over to The Knoll. He munched happily at a custard tart. The only cloud on his horizon was the prospect of another Daisy.

'I'll hire a good nanny,' he thought, quite forgetting that Daisy had gone through good nannies in short order. She had got through more good nannies than the agency had on its books. Indeed, had he known it, the name Daisy Parker had become a legend in nannying circles. Any prospective employer with the same surname was very carefully checked out indeed before even being interviewed.

Fortunately Uncle Parker had forgotten all this – or deliberately repressed it as too painful to recall. He fixed himself a gin and tonic and retired to the sitting room to finish reading the *Financial Times*.

Meanwhile back at Unicorn House tempers were frayed. Mrs Bagthorpe had returned to her room where she intended, she said, to draft the Rota and also certain House Rules.

'We must have a Strategy,' she said. 'We are in a State of Emergency.'

'When,' asked William bitterly, 'are we not?'

'You had better include Rosie and Grandma, Mother,' Tess told her. 'They'll be back tomorrow.'

'I shall include *everybody*,' said Mrs Bagthorpe. She meant her husband.

'And what about that tramp?' demanded William.

'Mr O'Toole is our guest,' she told him. 'He will not raise a finger. Where is he, by the way?'

'He went for a walk to the village,' Jack said. He thought it politic not to mention that he had seen Grandma slipping him the fiver.

'Are his clothes dry?' she asked, surprised.

'He went in that outfit you gave him. I think he quite fancies himself in it.'

'He certainly cuts an imposing figure,' she agreed.

Mr Bagthorpe now appeared, carrying his camera. He intended to photograph the milk bottles by the pool and the dead fish. Soon everyone had dispersed – William to compose his symphony for solo drum, Tess to embark on Molière and Mrs Bagthorpe to prepare her Rota. Only Jack and Zero, who had no Strings to their Bows, were left. The house began to reverberate to William's drumming.

'I expect he'll be up half the night composing his blasted symphony,' thought Jack. He sometimes swore in his thoughts, rarely out loud. This prospect for Jack, whose room was directly underneath his brother's, was unappealing. He had an inspiration.

'I know what, old chap,' he told Zero. 'We'll go camping. Just you and me.'

He immediately set about assembling his equipment. There was still plenty of fuel, purchased while they were in Wales, for his camping stove. In unconscious imitation of Uncle Parker he checked whether there were the ingredients for a good fry-up. There were. His spirits rose. In his short time on earth he had found few other joys to compare with that of bacon and eggs fried at dawn in a field with only Zero for company. Had he decided to write his own *Prelude* in the manner of Wordsworth, this experience would have merited several stanzas.

Jack did not intend to go far – only a couple of fields away. All the same, he would have to give notice of his intention. He went up and tapped on the door of his mother's room.

'Who's that?'

'It's Jack. Mother—'

'Oh, do go away! Please!' Mrs Bagthorpe was wrestling with her Strategy.

'But I only—'

'Go *away*!'

Jack shrugged.

'I'll leave a note,' he thought.

Lying on the kitchen table he found a buff envelope that looked like a bill for something. On it he scrawled 'Gone camping in Six Acre with Zero. Back tomorrow. Jack.'

He then propped this against the larger pepper mill and left. He went down the garden at the back of the house, followed by the sound of drums. By the time he was climbing the fence into the first field they had faded, leaving only the evening whistle of birds.

'Good old boy!' he told Zero, transferring his own feelings of delight. 'If there are any foxes in the night – you get them!'

Mrs Bagthorpe, her household reduced now only to four, if you counted Grandpa, was pitting her brains against her son's remorseless drumming. She had almost completed the Rota, and had tried to be scrupulously fair.

Everybody, in effect, had a turn at everything. This was a dangerous policy, as she knew from experience. She was well aware, for instance, that if someone particularly detested a certain chore, he or she would deliberately bungle it, in the hope of never being asked to do it again. Her own husband was the prime culprit. On one occasion, asked to do the washing, he had turned an entire load lime green, including William's tennis whites. When charged with this, he denied that he had done it on purpose, though his case was badly weakened by the fact that not one item of his own clothing had been included in the load. If asked to hoover, he would run the machine deliberately at pieces of string or scattered items of underwear, thereby sucking them up and clogging the works. He would then volunteer to take the Hoover into Aysham for repair, and stop there all day, well clear of the danger of being asked to do anything else.

'On this occasion he must be carefully supervised,' Mrs Bagthorpe told herself. 'I shall do so myself.'

In a desperate attempt to induce her family to view the whole thing in a playful light, she decided to draw up also a set of House Rules.

'I shall pretend that I am a landlady,' she thought. 'It will be a kind of game.'

She knew that on the rare occasions Mrs Fosdyke had been off ill, or visiting her cousin in Poges, the household had very soon gone into a downward spiral. Everybody waited for somebody else to do things like wash milk bottles and put them out, empty waste bins and so forth. In the end, of course, Mrs Bagthorpe herself had to do all these things. She did so with extreme resentment, while at the same time blaming herself that she had not brought up her offspring with a greater sense of responsibility.

'This will be an opportunity to train them,' she thought Positively, 'without their even realizing it.'

Half an hour or so later she had ready the first draft, which read as follows:

HOUSE RULES

1. Fire: arrangements are *ad hoc*, though it is to be hoped that anyone who notices the house burning down will notify others before saving his/her own skin. Use of barbecue forbidden on top floors between April and October.

2. The landlady reserves the right to refuse admission, to throw out without notice, and to up charges at her own discretion.

3. All beds to be made and vacated by 9 a.m.

4. Bathrooms to be left as you would hope to find them. Imminent running out of toilet paper to be NOTIFIED IMMEDIATELY.

5. Washing up. Dishwasher to be used when possible. Otherwise, this shall be deemed to mean the washing of all pots and utensils AND their drying, rather than being left for hours on end to air on the draining board. It also includes the wiping down of all associated surfaces, and the EMPTYING OF DIRTY DISHWATER in sink/ bowl.

6. Waste bin. This is not at the centre of a power

game in which all residents see how high they can pile it with refuse before the landlady finally cracks and empties it herself.

7. Ground floor and stairs to be hoovered daily. The Hoover bag is not at the centre of a power game in which all residents see how long they can use it before either (a) the landlady cracks and empties it herself, or (b) it bursts.

8. Milk bottles. The landlady does not, as some residents in the past have seemed to think, collect these. Nor does she enjoy tripping over half-washed clumps of these inside the back door.

9. Telephone. The landlady did buy a lock for this last year, but it has mysteriously gone missing. The telephone is only to be used for urgent calls, and even then only after obtaining the permission of the landlady. Calls describing what happened at last night's disco, or analysing the characters of friends, shall not be deemed urgent. The landlady reserves the right to listen in on all telephone conversations.

10. Late nights. Doors are normally locked at 10.30 p.m. and permission must be obtained by residents wishing to stay out later. Merrymakers returning past this hour, and wishing to prolong the evening with drinks of coffee/wine/ cocoa, should note that the landlady's bedroom is immediately above the kitchen.

Mrs Bagthorpe, feeling that ten was an appropriate number of Rules, as in the Ten Commandments, laid down her pen and read them through, smiling. No one else would do this. What she liked to think of as her gentle irony would meet with stony countenances from the rest of her family.

By now it was nearly dark, and Mrs Bagthorpe went downstairs in search of a restorative milky drink. In the kitchen she found her husband wolfing down a large portion of cold bread and butter pudding.

'Oh, there you are, Henry,' she greeted him. 'Will you join me in a cocoa?'

'You know perfectly well I won't,' he replied ungraciously, his mouth full. 'I am allergic to chocolate.'

'At least its consumption does not lead to cirrhosis of the liver,' his wife told him.

Before her spouse had time to think up a suitable rejoinder there came the sound of dragging footsteps and strangled groans.

'Oh – whatever?' cried Mrs Bagthorpe, and turned to see her elder son lurching through the doorway in patent agony.

'William! Whatever is the matter?'

He appeared not to hear her. He emitted low groans, clutched at his stomach and staggered past the dresser, thereby dislodging a Wedgwood plate that fell to the floor and smashed.

'Hell *fire*!' exclaimed Mr Bagthorpe, unmoved by his son's condition. 'Do you know what that thing was worth? Who d'you think's going to foot the bill for that?'

'Hush, Henry!' said his wife sharply. She hurried to William and attempted to draw him to a seat.

'Oh . . . oh . . .' he groaned. 'I'm dying . . .'

'Oh, but you're not, you mustn't!' cried his mother Positively. 'Tell me what has happened. Have you swallowed poison?'

'Poison . . .' William groaned.

'Bilge!' his father told him. Mr Bagthorpe could not bear to see other people taking centre stage. 'If anyone's poisoned around here, it's me!'

He shoved away his empty plate and stood up. As he did so, he caught sight of a buff envelope propped against the pepper mill. This acted as the proverbial red rag.

'What's this!' He snatched up the envelope, screwed it into a ball and hurled it towards the waste bin. 'Another final reminder! That's what's poisoning me! A remorseless flow of buff envelopes containing final demands, knee-deep in—'

Neither of the others was paying any attention to this often-before-played scene. William was concentrating on his own acting performance, which he felt was going well. His mother feeding him the word 'poison' had helped. He intensified his groans, and Mrs Bagthorpe began wringing her hands.

'Oh, what shall we do? Shall I ring for an ambulance?'

'No!' William was a shade too quick in his response, but she appeared not to notice. His idea was to be laid up for a few days in the summerhouse, picking at delicacies. Being hospitalized, and even operated on, was no part of his plan. He wondered where Jack had got to.

'I'm doing all the donkey work,' he told himself. 'All he's got to do now is fake a few twinges.'

'The doctor, then?' cried Mrs Bagthorpe.

'You leave that imbecile out of it,' her husband told her.

'I – I'll be all right!' William gasped, and gave what he hoped was a game smile. 'I think – the deep freeze . . . Jack . . .'

'Jack? On no! Of course, that dreadful deep freeze! Oh, I should never have asked you! Oh, where is Jack? Find him, Henry!'

'You find him!' came the terse rejoinder. Mr Bagthorpe stamped out, slamming the door.

'I – I think I'll go to bed!' William groaned.

He had intended to make himself a large ploughman's supper, complete with pickled onions, and then go to bed. Finding his parents in occupation of the kitchen had forced a rapid change of plan, and he felt he had coped well. He could always nip down and raid the pantry in the night, he reflected.

'Oh yes, do, darling,' his mother urged. 'You look very flushed!'

William notched this up as a further tribute to his acting skills. He had not known that he could act being flushed. Probably few could, he thought, as he staggered off.

'Probably not even Ben Kingsley,' he told himself. 'Or John Gielgud.'

He went off to bed, to lie and consider the possibility of adding acting as a further String to his Bow.

11

Mrs Bagthorpe, left alone in the kitchen, stood distraught, her mind going round in circles. At the centre of these circles was a vision of her younger son, lying pale and inert in some far flung corner of the house, or even the garden. She was herself in such a daze that she was brought to only by a violent hissing followed by the acrid smell of burnt milk.

'Oh! Oh!'

She had quite forgotten her restorative milky drink, and now had no stomach for it, especially burnt. She set off to search the house, calling, 'Jack, Jack! Answer me!' to the disgust of her spouse, who hammered loudly on the inside of his study door to indicate this.

Mrs Bagthorpe found that Breathing helped if she did it when she saw a crisis approaching, but once a downward spiral had begun usually forgot clean about it. In the present case she had been confronted by the anguished William before she had so much as had time to draw breath. As she went further up the house her cries grew increasingly frantic. William, lying in bed and picturing himself taking curtain calls at a Royal

Command Performance of *Hamlet*, smiled. Tess, on the other hand, flung open the door of her room and cried, 'Oh, shut up, Mother, do!'

'Oh, Tess, Tess! Jack is missing!'

'What d'you mean, missing? It's only just gone nine. He's probably off somewhere with that mutton-headed, pudding—'

'No!' her mother screamed. 'You don't understand!'

She started to explain, but was soon cut short.

'William?' echoed Tess disbelievingly. 'Ill? I bet he's not. He's just faking, to get out of doing things.'

'He is not!' returned her mother. 'He is quite desperately ill!'

William, listening, smiled the more and awarded himself an Oscar.

'Send for an ambulance, then,' said Tess. 'Get him to the hospital and let the experts decide.'

'Oh, should I? Do you think I should?'

This smartly wiped the smile off William's face.

'Oh, but Jack – Jack! Whatever has happened to him?'

'I hardly think that William's supposed indisposition has any relevance to the whereabouts of Jack,' Tess pointed out.

'Oh, but it does! The deep freeze! Salmonella! Poisoning!'

'Rats!' said Tess with commendable brevity, and slammed her door.

Mrs Bagthorpe roamed feverishly on, searching

even the attics for the unconscious body of her younger son. She then returned to the kitchen and put another pan of milk on the stove for another, by now much needed, restorative drink.

'He is not in the house. He must be lying somewhere in the garden,' she thought. 'We must send out a Search Party.'

Having formed this hazy notion, she soon realized its impractibility. The only other present occupants of Unicorn House were Grandpa, Tess, William and Mr Bagthorpe. Grandpa could be ruled out on account of his deafness and general slowness, and William on account of his condition. The remaining two, even if they could be commandeered, would form an exceedingly sketchy and reluctant Search Party.

Quite often in an emergency Mrs Bagthorpe would turn to Mrs Fosdyke, believing her to be a tower of strength.

'Oh, how I wish Mrs Fosdyke were on the telephone!' she thought now.

Even had this been the case, that lady, of course, was currently knocking back Guinness at the Fiddler's Arms, and basking in the reflected glory of her eccentric millionaire. She was far beyond the reach of any telephone.

Mrs Fosdyke was deeply suspicious of this instrument, and refused to have one in her house. This, Mr Bagthorpe maintained, was a ploy to use his own telephone free of charge, and save her own pocket. (There was some truth in this. Mrs Fosdyke would sometimes relieve her feelings by phoning her sister in Penge from her employer's house. Then, if anyone came along, she would slam down the receiver, saying loudly, 'That fish man don't deserve my custom!' or 'Haddock out of season, my elbow!' or some such thing, thus creating the impression that she had legitimately been ordering fish. On one occasion she had made such a remark *before* replacing the receiver. Her sister in Penge, alarmed by a sudden inconsequential reference to the price of skate, had rung straight back. Mrs Fosdyke had by then scooted back to the kitchen, and it had been Mr Bagthorpe who finally snatched up the receiver. No one knew what interchange then took place, but Mr Bagthorpe thereafter claimed that the caller had been a VAT Inspector, out to get him. The sister in Penge, for her part, now tended to believe Mrs Fosdyke when she claimed that her employers were mad.)

Be that as it may, Mrs Fosdyke did have a genuine mistrust of telephones, which she saw, from what the Bagthorpes could gather, as a kind of Trojan Horse.

'If I 'ad one, I'd know it was there,' she said. 'I'd know it was crouched there, waiting.'

She made it sound rather like a panther.

'And then again, 'alf the phones is bugged, nowadays,' she said. 'You could have the government listening to every word you said.'

When William pointed out that this was unlikely, given that Mrs Fosdyke was not a member of MI5, or a spy, she said darkly, 'It depends what they've got on you. Not all spies wear fur hats, you know. And then there's people ringing day and night with double glazing and kitchens. *I* ain't being woke at midnight with double glazing. And think what you'd have to pay, all them calls!'

Mrs Bagthorpe did try to explain that a charge was made only for outgoing calls, but Mrs Fosdyke could not be brought to see it.

'Incoming or out, what's the difference?' she argued. '*They* can't tell the difference.' (Meaning British Telecom.)

With this Mr Bagthorpe was inclined to agree. He often, he maintained, paid bills for the outgoing and incoming calls of every house in the village. Either that, he said, or one of his family was dictating Milton's *Paradise Lost* in instalments to someone in Australia.

Rosie said, 'But you could leave the phone off the hook, Mrs Fosdyke.'

She shuddered.

'What – and 'ave it *listening*?'

The Bagthorpes had given up. The chances of Mrs Fosdyke installing a telephone in her house were clearly just about on a par with the chances of her accommodating an alligator. Both, so far as she was concerned, bit.

Mrs Fosdyke, then, was incommunicado, and unavailable to be press-ganged into a manhunt.

'Where shall I turn?' Mrs Bagthorpe wondered,

briefly debating whether to phone the Samaritans. She decided against this.

'Some other tortured soul is in worse straits than myself,' she thought, without quite believing this.

She then, by some curious association of ideas, thought of the Parkers, who did not have any obvious affinity with the Samaritans, who surely did not spend their days swinging in white hammocks or, for that matter, swigging gin and tonic.

'Mother and Rosie will surely hurry back here when they learn of the crisis,' she thought optimistically. Mrs Bagthorpe liked to think the family were what she called 'closely knit', when in fact they were very loosely woven indeed. They would sometimes close ranks against a common enemy, but when it came to ordinary everyday living they were ruthlessly self-seeking, it was every man for himself.

When Mrs Bagthorpe gasped out her news to Uncle Parker he, at least, sounded concerned. He and Jack were old allies.

'So you think the poor chap might be lying somewhere senseless?' he asked.

This put the case in a nutshell, and Mrs Bagthorpe then begged him to come over, bringing Grandma and Rosie, to form a Search Party.

'Not Celia, of course,' she added. 'Not in her condition.'

It was hard to envisage Aunt Celia in any condition as a member of a Search Party. She almost certainly would not even have any suitable clothes. The picture of her sister-in-law in anorak and wellies actually caused Mrs Bagthorpe to emit a high-pitched giggle.

'Now easy does it, Laura,' said Uncle Parker. 'Leave the hysterics to Celia. Hang on while I go and tell the others.'

He went up to Daisy's room where he found the trio engaged in a noisy game of Snakes and Ladders. It was noisy because Grandma was, as usual, cheating. She cheated at everything, even when she played with Daisy, and had once been thrown out of a Bingo hall for attempting to influence the caller. At Snakes and Ladders she moved her counter up snakes and ladders alike, and refused to come down anything. By dint of these tactics she could win a game while the other players were still waiting to throw a six. (Grandma always threw a six first go. If the dice did not land to show six, she would nudge it with her sleeve until it did.)

Uncle Parker poked his head round the door, and the three of them looked up.

'Crisis at Unicorn House,' he announced. 'William's mortally ill, I gather, and young Jack's gone missing.'

'I have only to leave home for an hour and the whole household falls apart,' observed Grandma, using the distraction as a chance to push her counter swiftly up a few rows.

'Laura wishes us all to go and form a Search Party,' he told them.

'Oh, must we?' wailed Rosie. 'I haven't taken all my photos yet.'

'It is rather late at night for a person of my age to be roaming the garden with a flashlight,' said Grandma.

The only enthusiasm was shown by Daisy, who had a notoriously low threshold of boredom, and was certainly becoming bored of losing at Snakes and Ladders.'

'I like lookin',' she stated. 'I looked for dragons, din't I, Daddy?'

'Certainly you did, Daisy,' he affirmed. Then added with cunning, 'It is probable, of course, that Laura will have to call in the police.'

This effected an immediate and gratifying response.

'At my age I do feel the cold, but I could certainly put on my thermal underwear,' said Grandma, in an abrupt about-turn. 'Tell Laura to have it warmed and ready.'

'Right ho!' said Uncle Parker, and went to relay the news to his sister-in-law.

'They'll come,' he told her, 'though I'm afraid that means Daisy as well.'

'Of course! There's no harm in that!' cried the relieved Mrs Bagthorpe. Her memory must have been very short. All Daisy's previous visits to Unicorn House had included harm, some of it of a very serious order.

Uncle Parker went to inform his wife of the new development. He found her already in bed (a heavily draped four-poster) memorizing a few lines of Yeats, as she did every night before composing herself to sleep. She said that it put her at one with the universe.

'Darling Daisy is going forth on yet another quest,' she murmured, when apprised of the situation.

She did not, as might have been expected of a mother, express any fears on her child's behalf. She did not, for instance, moot the possibility of Daisy's falling head first in the darkness into a milk-curdled pool, full of dead fish with their ghastly, bloated mottled underbellies, etc.

'I wouldn't cross the road to find any of the rest of 'em,' Uncle Parker informed her, blowing a kiss. 'But poor old Jack's another matter. Pity Henry can't go missing.'

He went to collect his passengers and they all crowded again into his car.

'Hold tight!' he advised needlessly as he rolled out of his drive and started to scorch up the lane. When Uncle Parker drove, people always held tight. They frequently shut their eyes, too.

He screeched through the narrow lanes in his usual style, making no concession to the speed limit as he streaked through Passingham. He had just reached the outskirts when a pair of figures were picked out by his headlights. He slammed on his brakes, thereby dislodging Grandma's hat, and stopped a few inches short of what could justifiably be described as his targets.

'Good grief!' he exclaimed. 'It's Mrs F. and the old boy!'

It was indeed. Mrs Fosdyke and her millionaire were wending their way companionably homeward.

Mrs Fosdyke had confided in Mr O'Toole her fears about mass murderers in her wardrobe, and he had gallantly offered to escort her home. She had been enchanted by the prospect of her neighbours on Coldharbour Road seeing her come home on the arm of a millionaire, albeit one ostensibly wearing a nightdress.

It was not yet closing time. However the quartet in the Fiddler's Arms had been forced to cut the evening short by running out of funds. Mrs Fosdyke had emptied her purse. She was not, unlike Uncle Parker, the possessor of a gold American Express card, even had the landlord of the Fiddler's Arms heard of such a thing. (He recorded credit by the more direct and old-fashioned means of keeping a tally.)

Mrs Fosdyke did not believe in credit cards. To start with, she believed (here in unwitting agreement with Mr Bagthorpe) that the computers that ran them kept adding noughts on to everything. It was a known fact, she said. Most people who used credit cards eventually landed up in jail. Some of them never came out.

Then there were the credit-card robbers, as she called them. These were apparently a dedicated body of men whose sole aim in life was to steal other people's credit cards. There were no lengths to which they would not go to achieve this, including murder.

'Then they practise writing "G. Fosdyke" till they've got it off pat,' she said, 'and then they go out and buy hotels and jet planes and such. Then off they go to Barbados or somewhere leaving you to pay.'

Mrs Fosdyke did have an account at the Trustee Savings Bank. Once the manager had requested her to come and see him. He had, he explained, noted a tendency on her part to write very frequent cheques even on small transactions, such as the purchase of knitting needles, say. This, he had pointed out, was a very expensive way of doing things, and he had suggested a credit card.

Mrs Fosdyke had immediately launched into her views on this subject, while the bank manager listened spellbound. He had begun to wonder if he was in the right job. However, when the diatribe was over he tried to allay his client's fears, pointing out the various safety measures built into the system.

He must have been a very persuasive bank manager, and probably should have been a senior diplomat, because by the end of the interview Mrs Fosdyke had agreed to try both a credit and a Cashpoint card.

The consequences were unfortunate. Mrs Fosdyke, in her efforts to keep her credit card in a safe place as instructed, took to hiding it in all kinds of strange places which she then forgot. She did not, so far as was known, ever conceal it under the fourth lobelia from the left, but it was certainly once discovered by Jack in a packet of cornflakes.

The Cashpoint card presented even more serious problems. In his efforts to impress on his client the importance of never revealing her personal number to any other person, the bank manager had evidently overdone it.

'If your memory is unreliable, you may of course jot it down somewhere such as in your telephone book, disguised as a number,' he told her. 'But the best course is, as soon as the slip arrives, to memorize the number and then destroy the slip immediately.'

He did not in fact advocate swallowing the slip, as Mr Bagthorpe, in his determination that none of his family should know his number, had once done. But during the days she waited for her secret number to arrive Mrs Fosdyke had worked herself into a fair lather.

'I lay awake nights,' she confided in her employer, 'with figures darting round in my head like rats.'

When the sacred number finally arrived Mrs Fosdyke tore open the envelope with trembling fingers and stared with awe at the magical number that was hers and hers alone. It looked, she said, like no other number she had ever seen. At first she tried to memorize it, but each time found that after a few hours the number had vanished. She then hit upon the idea of entering it in her address book as a telephone number.

If she had left it at that, all might have been well. However she felt so strongly that that particular number stuck out like a sore thumb as a Cashpoint number, that she further elaborated the scheme. She decided first that she would enter it in more than one place, and secondly that each time she would transpose a couple of digits to disguise it. Well satisfied, she carried out this manoeuvre, and then ritually burnt the slip, placing it on a saucer to light it, and with unholy awe watching it brown, curl up and fall to ashes.

The result of all this was predictable. Within hours Mrs Fosdyke could not remember where exactly she had written the number, nor even what the digits had been, let alone in what order. She panicked. She took her best scissors and cut up her card so finely that it resembled mince. She then went to the Post Office, bought a registered envelope and addressed the shredded contents to the bank manager, with a note, saying: 'I, Gladys Fosdyke, solemnly swear that I do not know the number of the enclosed card and will never reveal it as long as I live.'

She posted it and went home satisfied, to have the first good night's sleep in ages. She woke refreshed, went straight to the oven where she had hidden her other card, and gave it exactly the same treatment.

Thus, then, when the cash ran out at the Fiddler's Arms, so had the Scotch and Guinness. Mr O'Toole and Mrs Fosdyke were in any case well oiled when they sallied forth. Finding themselves bathed in the full glare of Uncle Parker's headlamps, and only inches from his bumper, they turned and blinked with only mild surprise. They looked like a pair of benign owls.

Uncle Parker instantly leapt from his car and delivered his standard lecture to pedestrians who got in his path.

''E'd be going a hundred and fifty miles a minute,' Mrs Fosdyke told her companion sagely, and without malice. ''E always does.'

'There is an emergency,' said Uncle Parker sternly. 'Up at Unicorn House. We are a Search Party.'

'Ooooh!' exclaimed Mrs Fosdyke vaguely.

'We need every available person!' called Grandma from the car. She felt that Mrs Fosdyke's presence could only worsen an already bad scene. 'You had better hurry up there at once, both of you!'

'Oh, we shall, indeed we shall, ma'am,' promised Mr O'Toole, swaying gracefully. 'I'm in the way of being a first-class searcher. Spot a fag end in the gutter at twenty yards!'

Mrs Fosdyke tittered inanely at what she took to be a millionaire's merry quip, but what was, of course, a bald statement of fact. Mr O'Toole was also a very good spotter of saleable items thrown on rubbish dumps, and serviceable shirts on unattended washing lines. He had the true survivor's gift for spotting.

Uncle Parker jumped back into his car, hooted to clear the pedestrians smartly from his path, and careered on towards Unicorn House. There he narrowly missed running over his sister-in-law who was wandering about the drive waving a run-down torch.

In the kitchen they were all met by the stench of burnt milk, Mrs Bagthorpe having forgotten her second attempt at a restorative cocoa. Its power was such as to have brought Mr Bagthorpe out of his study.

'Hell fire, Laura,' he greeted his wife, 'can you not even boil a pan of milk?'

'If I cannot, then that places me in exactly the same category as yourself,' she returned icily. 'And during the coming weeks you will be able to practise doing so, since *I* shall certainly not be doing it.'

'Henry cannot even brew a pot of tea without incident,' observed Grandma. This was one of her favourite sayings. She seemed to forget that it was she who had brought him up unable to brew a pot of tea, boil an egg, hoover a carpet and so on.

'Oh, you're back, are you?' he said.

'An' me an' me an' me!' squeaked the excited Daisy. 'We goin' to look for dragons and Zacks!'

'Well, you can count me out,' said Mr Bagthorpe. 'And I advise you, Russell, to keep that crazed brat of yours well in your sights. I am currently engaged in writing to my lawyers, and damages are already high!'

With this he banged off back to his study, though even that was not the safe haven it had been, since Mrs Bagthorpe had pocketed the key. (She was later to drop it in the kitchen, where it would in turn be found and pocketed by Daisy Parker.)

12

William, who had heard Uncle Parker's car drive up, guessed that all the activity was on account of the missing Jack. He began to wonder whether he had overdone things. All the commotion was only because Jack was thought to be lying somewhere poisoned by the deep freeze. An ordinarily missing Jack would have occasioned only mild concern. In fact, it was unlikely that he would have been missed at all.

William toyed with the idea of going down and announcing his sudden miraculous recovery, but decided against it. He was pleased with his recent acting performance, and felt that he deserved a couple of days laid up in the summerhouse, where he could try to re-establish contact with Anonymous from Grimsby. After all, he himself knew that Jack was not poisoned, wherever he was.

Jack had pitched his tent at the far side of the Six Acre, under the chestnuts. He was sitting between the flaps, eating a packet of digestives and fondly watching Zero root about near by.

'You're a real hunter's dog,' he told him. 'I bet you're sniffing out moles. Good old chap!'

It was too dark to judge whether or not this praise brought Zero's ears up.

'You and me are outdoor types,' Jack went on. 'It's much better being here with the owls hooting than stuck up there with that lot and The Screechers.'

By this last he meant not another breed of owl, but Grandma's cracked singers of the Vienna State Opera Company, who were now thus alluded to in the Bagthorpe ménage. The sound of these was certainly sufficient to endanger anyone's health, and Jack was particularly worried that they might affect Zero. If so, what would be the cure? he wondered. And how would he describe to the vet exactly what the problem was? He decided that no words could do justice to it, and that his wisest course would be to take along one of Grandma's records and play it in the surgery.

Having made this decision he turned in for the night, blissfully unaware that a Search Party was out, and that he was meant, if and when found, to exhibit signs of acute poisoning. His last waking thoughts were of the bacon, eggs and mushrooms he would fry for breakfast in the dew.

Meanwhile, back at Unicorn House, Mrs Bagthorpe was organizing the Search Party.

'Me 'n' Daisy'll go together,' said Rosie. 'I'll fetch my torch.'

'It is to be hoped that darling Daisy does not fall into the pool,' said Grandma. 'We do not want any further fatalities.'

She made it sound as if Jack were already dead.

'Oh dear, oh dear!' cried poor Mrs Bagthorpe. She was already overcome with remorse at what she took to be her titanic failure as a mother. One son was lying upstairs in agony, and the other had vanished entirely. Both were victims of some terrible poison from the deep freeze, which she herself had ordered them to clear.

'I should have warned them of the dangers!' she thought. 'I should have insisted that they wore rubber gloves and washed their hands afterwards for five minutes with carbolic. I should never have exposed them to such danger. I should have done it myself!'

Grandma would have been highly gratified had she been able to read the thoughts running through the head of her daughter-in-law.

'I think I had better stay here and direct operations,' Grandma now said. What she really meant was that she wanted to be on hand when the police arrived. Also, as Search Director, she would be the one to decide when to call in the police. This she intended to be early on.

The searchers had more or less organized themselves when Mr O'Toole and Mrs Fosdyke made their entrance, blinking in the sudden light.

'Oh, Gladys, you have come!' Mrs Bagthorpe rushed forward and embraced her effusively. She seemed for a moment about to embrace the tramp, too.

'*I* requested her to come, Laura,' Grandma told her. 'It is a matter of life and death!'

'Death?' echoed Mrs Fosdyke, her hat rendered well askew by her employer's greeting. ''Oo's dead?'

She looked round the kitchen, noted to her disappointment that Daisy was still alive and kicking, and then, brightening, that Mr Bagthorpe was missing.

'Oooh – not Mr Bagthorpe?' she said.

'No one is dead, Mrs Fosdyke,' said Mrs Bagthorpe Positively. 'Not dead, but missing. Jack.'

'Oh – 'im!' remarked Mrs Fosdyke dismissively. 'And that great dog of 'is as well, I suppose. I'm wiping up after his great muddy paws morning noon and night. 'Ave *you* got a dog?'

This last was addressed to Mr O'Toole, who was mildly taken aback by the question. He did not know that Mrs Fosdyke believed him to be the owner of at least one country mansion, in the grounds of which she pictured him strolling, dressed in tweeds, with two Labradors at heel, or retrievers. He thought it was common knowledge that the Salvation Army does not encourage dogs.

'Er – no, dear lady,' he replied. 'Regrettably.'

'Oh, well, I suppose you can't, on account of the rabies,' Mrs Fosdyke told him. She also believed him to own estates in Jamaica, say, or the Caribbean, and imagined him jetting back and forth between them. 'You wouldn't want him 'alf his life in quarantine.'

Here she lost him entirely. By and large the Salvation Army ran a very good hostel, and the only risk, so far as he knew, was of fleas, to which he had often himself been host. Nobody had ever mentioned rabies.

Mrs Bagthorpe tried to press the matter in hand. Valuable seconds were ticking by.

Her eye was caught by her husband, lurking in the background.

'You, Henry, had better lead one party,' she told him.

'Why had I?' he demanded.

'Because you are Jack's father, of course.'

'I sometimes wonder,' he said. 'That boy's brains rattle round in his skull like tapioca. If he's going to go missing, why cannot he leave a note to say so? If he'd had the sense he was born with, he'd've left a note, and then we would not be milling about in the dark like some blood-crazed posse out of a Western.'

He was later to regret this statement. When it turned out that he himself had been responsible for screwing up Jack's note, he tried to bluff his way out of it.

'No one in his right mind would use a buff envelope for a note,' he said. 'Buff envelopes were made to be screwed up and tossed into bins. I did what anybody would've done.'

In the end Mr Bagthorpe did stamp bad-temperedly into the garden, yelling, 'Where are you? Come out from wherever you're skulking, you hear me? Where the blazes are you?'

He sounded a far cry from a distraught father.

'I bet he goes straight round the house and in again

at the front door and back into his study,' said Rosie, and no one contradicted her. 'Come on, Daisy, I'll take the batteries out of my Walkman and put them in my torch.'

'I'll wander out there and take a look myself, Laura,' offered Uncle Parker. 'Got a torch in the car.'

Gradually the kitchen emptied as one by one they embarked on the search for a Jack who was indeed lying unconscious, but blissfully so, in his tent under the chestnuts. Mr O'Toole obligingly padded back into the night and took a prowl through the shrubbery, occasionally calling, 'Johnny, Johnny boy, are ye there?'

Soon the only occupants of the kitchen were Grandma and Mrs Fosdyke. Grandma was twitchy, itching for her cue to dial 999. Mrs Fosdyke was vague and uncharacteristically fond and sentimental.

''E was a lovely boy,' she said, meaning Jack. This was far removed from her usual estimate of Jack, and Grandma darted her a sharp look.

'A proper little gentleman,' went on Mrs Fosdyke, 'though where he got it from's a mystery. Not his father. Even when he was ever so little you could see 'e'd a lovely nature. I can see 'im now, lying there in his pram twanging that string of blue plastic ducks he had and beaming up for all the world like Ramona Lisa.'

Grandma was becoming irritated by these maudlin reminiscences. Also, she did not like the way Jack was being referred to in the past tense. She herself was fond of Jack, in her own way, though would never have admitted to it, even under torture.

'Should you not be out there looking for Jack, Mrs Fosdyke?' she asked. 'After all, Mr O'Toole is, and he is a complete stranger.'

''E's a lovely man,' said Mrs Fosdyke, off on a new tack. 'A proper gentleman. They could see that, even in the Fiddler's. And do you know—'

'If you are not up to the search,' interrupted Grandma, 'perhaps you should busy yourself with refreshments for the Search Party on their return.'

Mrs Fosdyke considered this suggestion, then nodded. She looked about her for a moment and then, still wearing her coat and hat, meandered into the pantry.

The shrieks that followed were impressive even by Bagthorpian standards. One would have imagined that at the very least Mrs Fosdyke was confronted by a headless corpse. What she had actually encountered, of course, were two stags' heads and a bucketful of dead goldfish, with their vast, greenish, mottled bloated underbellies, etc.

Grandma froze. Then, like a flash, she was headed for the hall and dialling 999. She made the call and slammed down the receiver. Away in the distance, Mrs Fosdyke was still screaming on one eerie, high-pitched note, as if a needle had stuck. She could have successfully auditioned for the cracked Vienna State Opera Company. She would probably even have landed one of the leads.

The study door was flung open.

'Who've you been ringing?' Mr Bagthorpe demanded. 'And who's making that unholy racket?'

'The police,' Grandma told him. 'Mrs Fosdyke.'

'The—? Are you mad? A numb-skulled idiot and
his matted-up dog go for a walk and you send for the
police?'

'Go and save Mrs Fosdyke,' Grandma ordered.
'And you had better slap her face.'

'Slap it yourself!' he told her, and went back into
his study.

Grandma was at a loss. She did not know about the
stags and the dead fish in the pantry. For all she knew,
Mrs Fosdyke *had* encountered a headless corpse, and
worse, the perpetrator of this crime. Grandma was not
a coward, but she did take very good care of herself,
particularly her legs and fingernails. The idea of being
decapitated, and even dismembered, did not appeal.
She wisely judged that there was little she could do
faced with a homicidal maniac. She retreated to her
room. There she put on a record of the Valkyries, to
drown out the screaming downstairs, and waited for
the police to arrive.

When they did, a few minutes later, they were
confronted by a situation as baffling as any they had
yet encountered. As it happened, they were the same
pair who had been called to Coldharbour Road the
previous night, which had been their most baffling
case to date. Now they were doubly baffled.

On their way up the drive their headlamps picked

out the towering figure of Mr O'Toole in his long frock.

'That looked like a lunatic,' observed One. 'A big one. We'd better get to the house first, and get put in the picture.'

With any luck, he reflected, they could spend a long time taking statements, by which time the big lunatic would have got clear. He had little idea that they were heading straight into a nest of lunatics.

They drew up in front of the house, and the first thing they saw was Mr Bagthorpe, silhouetted against the light in his study, jumping up and down and shaking his fists. They did not at this time recognize him as their assailant of the previous night. Their impulse was to stay put in their vehicle, and radio for reinforcements. In the end they did get out of the car, but not until they had radioed for urgent assistance.

'There are at least two dangerous lunatics at large,' they told the Control Room.

As they climbed nervously out of their vehicle, looking left and right, the first thing they heard was the Valkyries. The effect of this sound, drifting over a darkened English garden, was unnerving. It was certainly such as to make the police officers think that they had seriously underestimated the number of dangerous lunatics at large.

They raised their eyes towards what seemed to be the source of the screeching, and saw the fiercely gesticulating figure of Grandma, at her window. At this point they nearly dived for the car.

They were forestalled by the appearance of yet another lunatic, a little one this time, from the rear of the house, making for them at a fast lick. Mrs Fosdyke was off home, where she intended to stay indefinitely, mass murderer in the wardrobe or not. When she saw the flashing blue light of the police car she made for it like a homing pigeon.

'It's 'orrible, 'orrible!' she screamed, as she had been doing for the past five minutes. 'It's 'orrible, 'orrible!'

'Er – what is that, madam?' inquired Two nervously, flicking his eyes about.

'In my pantry! All dead and 'orrible! Ugh!'

She shuddered. The officers exchanged glances.

'Three of 'em!' Mrs Fosdyke screamed. 'Three four five!'

The policemen recognized her as the party in Coldharbour Road who believed a mass murderer to be out to get her. It now began to seem all too possible that she might have been right.

'Er – how many?' asked One, who had no way of knowing that Mrs Fosdyke was referring not to bodies, but goldfish.

''Orrible! Ugh! 'Orrible! I don't know – three four five—!'

At this point a childish treble piped up out of the darkness.

> 'One two free four five
> Once I caught a fishy live!'

The police whirled about, playing their torches. There was Daisy Parker, ringlets tousled, cheeks flushed from the chase. She beamed at them. (Daisy liked the police, and mistakenly believed that they liked her. She had destroyed more squad cars than any other person since records began. The Bagthorpes thought she probably rated an entry in the *Guinness Book of Records* on this account. They did not propose her, because they were in there themselves for the Longest Daisy Chain in the World, and would brook no competition.)

'We lost Zack!' she squealed. 'We playin' Lickle Bo Peep and Hunt the Sipper!'

The police, who took the last word to be Ripper, wondered at what age people could be classified as lunatics. This was certainly the youngest they had so far encountered.

'Zack might be *dead*!' she now confided, saucer-eyed. Then, apparently inconsequentially, 'All the bees are dead!'

The police were just mulling over this last statement when Grandma appeared, closely followed by Tess.

'Oh, there you are, Mrs Fosdyke!' exclaimed the former. 'I thought you had been murdered.'

'What's up?' demanded Tess. She had resisted coming down to discover the reason for the return of Uncle Parker and his guests, but her curiosity had now got the better of her.

''Oo's going to go and get them dead things out

my pantry!' wailed Mrs Fosdyke. 'One two three four five—'

'Once I caught a fishy live!' Daisy again obligingly supplied.

There came a loud banging on the study window, and everyone turned to see Mr bagthorpe's frantic silhouette.

'Er – who is that?' inquired One, taking out his notebook. He felt that he must make a start somewhere.

'That, officer, is my son,' Grandma told him. 'He cares not a fig that his younger son is missing, presumed dead.'

'Why is he banging on the window?' asked Two. 'Perhaps he requires assistance?'

'He is banging on the window because he wishes to obstruct you in the course of your inquiries,' replied Grandma. 'Do not allow yourselves to be deflected.'

'Go 'way, Uncle Bag!' squealed Daisy. She picked up a chubby fistful of gravel, ran forward and flung it against the study window. Mr Bagthorpe rapidly retreated out of view.

'There!' exclaimed Grandma, triumphant. 'That is the way to deal with Henry!'

She looked at the police as if challenging them to throw handfuls of gravel, too.

'If Jack really is missing,' said Tess, 'why is nobody looking for him?'

She looked directly at the police.

'Er – there are other more urgent matters,' said One.

'Oooh, in my pantry,' moaned Mrs Fosdyke.

Two cleared his throat.

'We had better go and investigate,' he said.

Neither officer was keen to do this, and the arrival on the scene of Uncle Parker and Mrs Bagthorpe provided a welcome delay.

'Oh, officers,' sobbed Mrs Bagthorpe. 'Thank heaven you have come!'

Dishevelled as she was, the police recognized her. Uncle Parker they knew well. His driving was frequently reported, though they had never yet managed to arrest him.

'Evening, officers,' he greeted them. 'Foiled again, I fear!'

'We are not investigating motoring offences, sir,' One told him stiffly.

'Which are a serious waste of police time,' added Two.

'Glad to hear you say so,' said Uncle Parker. 'My own view entirely.'

'Where are the others?' cried Mrs Bagthorpe, looking wildly about her. 'Where are the dogs and divers?'

The police looked askance at this. Grandma's phone call had not referred to any missing person. It had simply informed them that someone was being murdered.

'You must comb the grounds inch by inch!' Mrs Bagthorpe told them. 'Ah – here are the others!'

A flashing blue light was visible among the trees lower

down the drive. If Mrs Bagthorpe was relieved, the two policemen were even more so. Daisy, predictably, was ecstatic (as was Grandma, though she took good care to hide it).

'Here's some more blue twinklies!' squeaked Daisy. 'I goin' to talk to invisible mans!'

The two policemen did not recognize this remark as being ominous. They had no way of knowing that what Daisy was referring to was the two-way radio. While in Wales, she had been left unattended with one of these, and had practically the entire Welsh police force on red alert.

'Ah, good!' said One heartily. He was beginning to feel outnumbered, if not actually oppressed, by Bagthorpes. 'Here are the reinforcements. We can now conduct a thorough search of the house.'

'But I've already searched the house!' cried Mrs Bagthorpe.

'You never searched *my* house,' said Mrs Fosdyke jealously. '*And* you never sent reinforcements. I told you to send for reinforcements, but oh no, you knew better. If I was to've been—'

'Oh, do be *quiet*!'

Mrs Bagthorpe forgot herself. She forgot Mrs Fosdyke's nerves and her Occasional Thurpy. She forgot who was likely to end up doing all the washing, ironing, dusting, scrubbing . . . She remembered too late.

'Oh, do forgive me, Gladys!' she pleaded. 'It's simply that—'

The reinforcement police were now bearing down on the group.

'Now – what's it all about?' demanded Three.

'Oh – have you brought the dogs and divers?' Mrs Bagthorpe looked about her for evidence of these.

'Dogs and *divers*?' repeated Four. 'What dogs? What divers?'

From above came a tortured, regular screeching. The needle had stuck on the Valkyries.

And then the explanations began.

13

The disgust of the officers when they found they had been summoned to deal with dead stags and goldfish was extreme. There was a good deal of muttering about wasting police time, and possible prosecutions for this. They had, they felt, been made to look extremely silly. They had, after all, first surrounded the pantry and then approached it, with a caution that would have suggested a Mafia godfather holed up in there with his relatives. If they had been equipped with firearms, they would have used them.

As the four of them stood gaping at the bucket of dead goldfish Daisy ran past them to embrace her missing pets.

'Oh, *der* you are, darling Grandpa Gruffs!' she squealed. 'You coming to my house!'

'And what about the fish?' inquired Mr Bagthorpe, who had emerged from his study in order to bait the police. 'Taking them as well are you, Russell?'

''Oo *put* them there?' Mrs Fosdyke demanded. 'That's what I should like to know. Dead fish don't walk.'

'Nor live ones,' murmured Uncle Parker.

As Jack was not there to explain his attempt at resuscitation, all eyes went inevitably to Daisy. Mrs Fosdyke advanced towards her pantry, now sniffing noisily.

'And what's that I smell?' Sniff sniff! 'Brandy! 'Oo's been at my brandy?'

All eyes went now to Mr Bagthorpe, as the most obvious culprit.

'I have not yet come to sipping brandy in pantries,' he said coldly. 'Though I'm not surprised that she has.'

He meant Mrs Fosdyke, to whom he never spoke directly if he could help it. She was now bent double over the bucket of goldfish and sniffing for all she was worth.

'It's in there!'

She pointed dramatically. The plot was thickening by the moment. Nobody underestimated Daisy Parker's inventive powers and originality. Nobody even pretended to know the way her mind worked. But to lug a bucket full of dead goldfish from the curdled pond, conceal them in Mrs Fosdyke's pantry and then dose them liberally with brandy seemed, even by Daisy's standards, an awe-inspiringly original act. It made Monty Python, as Mr Bagthorpe later said, look like a party political broadcast. He said this even after it transpired that Jack had done it.

'He may not be a genius,' he declared, 'but at least he can have a stab at being eccentric. Anyone can.'

The four police clearly found the situation very eccentric indeed.

''Ooever'd pour good brandy into a bucket of dead fish?' wondered Mrs Fosdyke, speaking for all present. She shook her head, tottered over to a chair, sat down and looked as if she was preparing for sleep.

'And talking of brandy,' said Mr Bagthorpe, 'where's that stinking brute that swilled my malt whisky?'

'Yes, where is the old boy?' said Uncle Parker. 'Passed him earlier, with Mrs F . . .'

'You didn't exactly pass him, Uncle Park,' Rosie told him. 'You practically ran him down.'

'Still wearing his best frock,' continued Uncle Parker.

At this the first two policemen pricked up their ears. They had understandably forgotten about the big lunatic they had passed in the drive. A lot had happened since to take their minds off him.

'Ah,' said One. 'Is this the missing person?'

'No, it is not!' said Mrs Bagthorpe passionately. 'My son, my younger son, is the missing person. Mr O'Toole simply went looking for him.'

'Ah, and himself went missing as a result,' said Two, with the air of one putting two and two together and coming up with a very sinister result.

'I believe we sighted the person on our approach,' said One. 'We took him for a lunatic.'

'He's that, all right,' Mr Bagthorpe told them. 'And a dipsomaniac to boot.'

'He was certainly wearing very odd attire,' said One.

'It is not odd at all,' said Mrs Bagthorpe coldly. 'It is mine.'

'For a *gentleman*,' Two corrected himself hastily. 'Does the person in question often attire himself in female clothing? Why was he wearing your frock, madam?'

'I'll tell you why,' said Mr Bagthorpe. 'Because his own things stank to high heaven. That's why.'

'Just one moment, officers,' put in Grandma swiftly. 'Would you please step outside with me? I have confidential information to impart.'

She went into the hall, and the four policemen obediently followed. People did tend to go along with Grandma. She had a naturally authoritative manner, she said.

'My son, officers,' she told them, 'is, as you can see, unhinged.'

The quartet nodded sagely. They thought they could see.

'He will try to tell you that the missing gentleman is a common vagrant,' she continued. 'In fact, he is an eccentric millionaire. An old friend of my husband's.'

'Ah!' exclaimed One, as if light were beginning to dawn.

'Hence the attire!'

He talked as if the tabloids were plastered daily with photographs of Paul Getty and Richard Branson wearing frocks.

'Precisely!' nodded Grandma. 'The only other person in the house privy to this information is Mrs Fosdyke, who is the only one to be trusted.'

Mrs Fosdyke had not so far struck the police as notably trustworthy, but they refrained from saying so.

'Everyone else will say that Mr O'Toole is a tramp, because this is what they believe to be true,' Grandma went on. 'It is, of course, a serious matter when a millionaire goes missing.'

The police began to look worried. They certainly did not want a missing millionaire on their patch.

'One has to think in terms of kidnapping,' Grandma said. 'And ransom notes. It is to be hoped that we do not receive his ear in the post, or some of his fingers.'

At this juncture Grandpa appeared. He had glimpsed the flashing blue lights in the drive, and was drawn towards them as a moth to a flame. Grandpa was a man who took pleasure in the simple things of life, flashing blue lights being one of these.

'Ah, Alfred!' Grandma greeted him. 'How timely. You can confirm my story to the officers.'

'What was that?' inquired Grandpa, obviously having thrown his switch to the SD mode at the sight of his wife.

'I was saying that Mr O'Toole is a great friend of yours!' Grandma spoke very loudly and distinctly.

'Oh – yes!' He beamed. 'Where is he?'

'There is no need for us to alarm him,' hissed

Grandma, *sotto voce* to the police. 'He is, as you can see, old and frail.' She raised her voice. 'Just gone for a little walk, dear. He will be back shortly.'

'Ah – good, good!' Grandpa nodded amicably at the four officers and ambled off to inspect their squad cars.

'You must act fast!' Grandma told the police. 'Every second is vital!'

She now had them thoroughly wound up. They held a hasty conference and decided to make an immediate and thorough search of the garden.

'We'll get the dogs in,' said One.

Grandma went back to the kitchen.

'They are sending for the dogs, Laura,' she informed her daughter-in-law.

'Oh, thank you, Mother!' Mrs Bagthorpe mistakenly believed that Grandma had been drumming up concern for Jack. 'What about the divers?'

'You seem pretty well off for searchers now, Laura,' said Uncle Parker. 'I rather think I'll shoot off. Can't leave Celia for too long.'

This the Bagthorpes knew to be true. Unless actually asleep, Aunt Celia needed Uncle Parker constantly at hand, to support and cherish her.

'If ever Russell kills himself in that car,' Mr Bagthorpe would say, 'as he certainly will, sooner rather than later, Celia will keel over like a string of dominoes.'

'Darling Daisy shall stay here with me,' said Grandma.

'Good-o!' said Uncle Parker. He had managed, as

usual, to off-load Daisy. He was, on the other hand, genuinely concerned about Jack.

'Give me a buzz the minute you find him,' he told Mrs Bagthorpe. 'Poor old chap.'

He usually thought of Jack in these terms, gone missing or not. He sympathized with him on account of his family.

'Off you go,' Mr Bagthorpe told him. 'Make sure Celia hasn't fallen out of her hammock. There is one thing, a good bang on the head won't do *her* any harm! Ha!'

Uncle Parker had intended to scoop up the stags' heads on his way out and make off with them, but was prevented by his daughter. Daisy had temporarily dumped them while poking round the bucket of goldfish, but her gimlet eyes spotted the manoeuvre.

''Top it, 'top it, Daddy!' she squealed. 'Leave dem! Dey's going sniffin' after Zack!'

'You heard her, Russell,' said Mr Bagthorpe. 'Drop 'em!'

Uncle Parker did so, and made his getaway. In the brief silence that followed his exit there was a loud snore. Mrs Fosdyke's head had dropped right back, her mouth was ajar. The combination of Guinness and shock had sent her right off.

The Bagthorpes stared at her with open distaste.

'Bless her!' said Mrs Bagthorpe vaguely.

'*Bless?*' Mr Bagthorpe was disgusted. 'If it weren't for her, my life would be an idyll. Who landed me with half the policemen in the county?'

'I did, Henry,' Grandma reminded him. 'Are you going to search for your son?'

'No,' he replied. 'I am not. He'll turn up. He always has before. Let the *police* make monkeys of themselves!'

Mr Bagthorpe was not as a rule strong on prescience, but here, for once, he hit the nail bang on the head. Jack would have turned up, and the police *did* make monkeys of themselves. The only people who did not were Mr Bagthorpe himself and Grandma. (Mrs Fosdyke was unconscious in her chair for most of the night, and William was lying in bed poisoned.)

It was a busy night. The first real snag came up when the tracker dogs arrived. It was easy enough to find one of Jack's socks to give them his scent. In Mr O'Toole's case there were complications. The clothes he had taken off before his bath would certainly have provided a scent – probably enough to knock the tracker dogs unconscious. These however, thanks to Mrs Fosdyke's ministrations, were in the washing machine.

'Give 'em a sniff of Scotch,' Mr Bagthorpe advised the handlers. 'Tell 'em to follow that!'

This, given that Mr O'Toole did not, as far as was known, sprinkle Scotch on his feet, was a non-starter.

The only sighting of the tramp had been in the drive, and so many people (including the police themselves) had been milling around there since that the dogs would be thrown into hopeless confusion.

The result of this was that Jack was found early on, but the police were left with a missing millionaire.

They were understandably disgusted when Jack was found, complete with provisions, snugly rolled up in his tent. Jack, waking to find himself in eyeball to eyeball contact with a large Alsatian, naturally thought he was dreaming. He turned over and tried to get back to sleep, but found his tent unaccountably brightly lit. He sat up, blinking in the glare.

'What's up?' he asked. 'Where's Zero?'

Zero had shot off into the spinney. He was frightened of other dogs. He was frightened of miniature poodles, let alone police Alsatians. It was a long while before he could be coaxed out. He lay under a clump of brambles, only the whites of his eyes showing. This, Jack stoutly maintained, went to show how intelligent he was.

'It was his way of protecting me,' he told everybody. 'He would have come out and taken everyone by surprise. He'd've waited till the Alsatians were too busy sniffing to notice, then come out and got them. Good old chap!'

The Bagthorpes remained unconvinced by this explanation of Zero's strategy. They had all, at one time or another, seen him being chased by cats, let alone dogs, and did not believe him capable of even the simplest strategy.

'He's much too thick to have thought all that out,' Rosie told Jack. 'You know he is.'

In the event the police had to leave Jack still trying

to coax Zero out of the brambles while they returned to the house to report that he was found. By then, Daisy Parker had gone missing.

News of Jack's safety was brushed aside by almost everyone except his mother.

'Daisy was placed in your charge. You were her guardian,' Grandma told poor Rosie, who was, after all, only eight herself. 'She is out there somewhere in the darkness, and I, her old grandmother, must go out in search of her. I shall have no rest until she is found.'

She made it sound like something out of *King Lear*.

'I only went to the loo!' wailed Rosie. 'Oh, poor little Daisy – come on, come on everybody, *find* her!'

The police were now torn between searching for a missing four-year-old and a multimillionaire. They knew that their failure to find either would attract very unwelcome headlines in the tabloids, and seriously jeopardize their chances of promotion.

'All we can hope for,' said one dog-handler, 'is that we'll find one while looking for the other.'

In this he was to be disappointed. This was because of an event unprecedented in police records. The tracker dogs themselves went missing.

They were led to the stags' heads, recently so warmly embraced by Daisy, to get her scent. They seemed thrown by this. The stags' heads had very big, staring eyes, and the Alsatians stiffened as they approached and made soft rumbling growls. Zero had probably had the right idea in heading for the spinney. If the stags were able, *they* probably would have headed for the spinney.

Once the dogs had had a good sniff, their handlers decided that as they were searching private grounds, they could now be unleashed to do their tracking.

'They'll have her in no time, madam,' Handler One told Grandma. 'Can't have got far on those little legs.'

The Bagthorpes, who had reason to know how fast the little legs in question could move, were sceptical. Even they, however, could not have guessed that the dogs would vanish into thin air, along with Daisy herself.

While the dogs were searching, Mrs Bagthorpe made coffee and distributed it to the grateful officers. Mrs Fosdyke's unconscious and gently snoring presence was maddening.

'Look at her!' said Rosie. 'Whenever things get tough she just cops out!'

'Try forcing some of that stuff down her throat, Laura,' Mr Bagthorpe advised. 'And make it hot. If her tongue gets scalded it might shut her up for a few days. Ha!'

His wife gave him a quenching look, but the police, thinking that Mr Bagthorpe was joking, laughed. He then gave *them* a quenching look.

'Did you have to pass tests to get into the force?' he asked them. 'Intelligence tests?'

They assured him that they did.

'Good grief!' he said. 'I suppose that means anybody could get in. Perhaps Jack could, Laura. He could take that lumpy mutton-headed hound with him. And talking of dogs, shouldn't you be tagging on after yours? If they find a corpse, they could've eaten it by the time you get there.'

The handlers, who by rights should have stayed with their animals, put down their coffee and thanked Mrs Bagthorpe. They then went out to track their trackers. Rosie was already out there alone, by the pool, stirring the curdled water with a rake while tears ran down her cheeks.

'Daisy!' she called forlornly from time to time. 'Daisy!'

Where Daisy was was in the potting shed, with the police Alsatians. She had trotted out into the garden unobserved and with no clear intentions. As far as she was concerned the night was still young and she still had energy to discharge. She usually had. Mr Bagthorpe said that she had more stored energy than Battersea Power Station.

'If you plugged her in, you could light up London,' he stated.

Lately, he had begun to liken her to Windscale, and said she was probably radioactive.

'She is certainly a danger to health,' he said, and this was unarguable.

When Daisy lighted on the potting shed she stopped in her tracks. She had forgotten about it, but had once had a very creative session in there, mixing up together all Mrs Bagthorpe's flower and vegetable seeds. The garden had had a very original, not to say surreal, aspect that season. Seeing it now, nestled among the trees, it struck her as resembling the hut in the forest where Hansel and Gretel had sheltered. It was not, unfortunately, made of gingerbread, but with any luck, she thought, it might harbour a witch.

Daisy Parker was not frightened of witches or hobgoblins or dragons or trolls or any of the things four-year-olds are supposed to be frightened of. In fact, she tended to identify with them, and got disappointed when stories always ended with their getting their come-uppance.

'Poor lickle wolf!' she would sigh at the end of Red Riding Hood, and 'Why don't that silly Hansel and Gretel get cooked instead of that nice lickle ole witch!'

Daisy stood on tiptoe to lift the latch, and as she did so was joined by the two police dogs. They had after all been given the stags' heads to sniff, and had probably followed her scent as being the strongest. She certainly rarely consented to being bathed.

'Oooh!' she exclaimed. 'Wolfs! Come on, wolfs, nice wolfs!'

The door swung open and she trotted in, followed by the Alsatians. Daisy then closed the door behind them. They prowled about the shed, sniffing. Daisy was enchanted. She would make them her pets, she decided, mentally adding them to her existing menagerie of Billy Goat Gruff and the stags' heads. She dug around her person for a bar of chocolate, which she then fed to them. They licked their lips in a thoroughly wolf-like way.

'I in't Wed Widing Hood,' she told them. 'So dat's all wight.'

She could make out their bright, questing eyes in the gloom.

'We'll play Womlus and Wemus,' she told them. 'I'll lie down, and you keep me warm.'

She accordingly curled up on a heap of sacks, which she then patted invitingly. The two Alsatians, having so far as they were concerned found their quarry, obligingly lay too.

Daisy lay contentedly pushing her chubby fingers into their thick coats. She was in very heaven. She wondered drowsily whether her luck was really in, and these were not merely wolves, but werewolves. If so, there would never again be a moment's boredom, the world would at a stroke become a paradise. One hand moved slowly from the dense coat of her werewolf, a pudgy finger found her mouth and then Daisy Parker, smiling blissfully, was asleep.

14

It was Uncle Parker who, quite effortlessly, found Mr O'Toole. Uncle Parker usually achieved things effortlessly, or at any rate gave the appearance of doing so.

Mr O'Toole, finding himself wandering about the shrubbery of Unicorn House without fully understanding why, had experienced a sudden, overpowering uprush of his vagrant instincts. He had spent too long under the same roof. His feet, encased in their Afghan slipper socks, itched.

He tended to avoid roads, and struck off across the fields, in the very direction Jack had himself taken earlier. He was taking, without knowing it, the crow's flight route to The Knoll. By the time he reached it he was in need of a rest. He sat down, leaned his back against Uncle Parker's automatic gates, and nodded off.

His awakening was rude. Uncle Parker had very strong headlights, as indeed he needed to have.

'Good grief!' exclaimed Uncle Parker. 'It's the old boy!'

He thought fast. The public-spirited thing to do

would be to coax Mr O'Toole into his car and return him to Unicorn House, thus saving the police a fruitless search. Uncle Parker, however, did not feel like saving the police a fruitless search. They were always trying to arrest him for his driving. He owed them no good turns. Also, Uncle Parker liked colourful characters and eccentrics. (He was, after all, married to one.)

He jumped out, helped Mr O'Toole to his feet, and led him to the car.

'Hop in!' he said. 'We're nearly there.'

'Nearly there,' repeated Mr O'Toole amiably, and got in.

He had barely closed his eyes when the car drew up outside the house.

'Are we already there?' He seemed only mildly surprised. 'Is this the hostel?'

Uncle Parker assured him that it was. Mr O'Toole appeared to accept the panelled hall and suits of armour, but must have wondered when Uncle Parker offered him a Scotch as night cap (to ensure that he went straight off without disturbing Aunt Celia). In his experience, the Salvation Army did not dispense Scotch, even at Christmas. However, he awarded this particular hostel a five-star rating, and allowed himself to be led up to a spare room.

'Lucky you've got your nightie on already,' Uncle Parker told him. 'Sleep well!'

He shut the door on the visitor and went blithely off, humming 'While Shepherds Watched' under his breath. (When in good humour Uncle Parker often hummed carols, however unseasonal. He said the tunes were too good to be wasted for eleven months out of the twelve.)

He found his wife sleeping peacefully, a faint smile on her lips. He then turned in himself. As he lay there, he pictured the beleaguered Bagthorpes and police, searching fruitlessly through the night. Soon, all three members of the Parker family were sleeping peacefully, a faint smile on their lips.

Meanwhile smiles, faint or otherwise, were thin on the ground at Unicorn House. The police, having lost their dogs, became as near hysterical as trained police officers could ever be. Tess started expounding theories of Black Holes, and talking about the Bermuda Triangle.

'Inexplicable disappearances are legion,' she told the police. 'Modern society assumes that if a thing is lost, it can be found. This is a fallacy, a manifestation of hubris. What happened to the crew of the *Flying Dutchman*? Where are all the aeroplanes that vanished in the Bermuda Triangle?'

'And Anonymous from Grimsby,' put in Rosie. 'He's gone missing as well.'

'As soon as we know for certain that everyone has vanished for good, I shall register the incident,' Tess said. 'This may well become known as the Bagthorpe Triangle.'

'Bilge,' said Mr Bagthorpe. 'If this was a Triangle worth its salt, *she* would have disappeared long ago.'

He meant the gently snoring Mrs Fosdyke.

As the night wore on, the existence of a Bagthorpe Triangle began to look increasingly likely.

'It beats me,' said Handler One morosely. 'A millionaire, a child and two police dogs, all mysteriously gone missing. It must break all existing records.'

'It will certainly give the tabloids a field day,' agreed Mr Bagthorpe, voicing the Handler's own secret fears. 'I can see the headlines now: MAD MILLIONAIRE AND MOPPET MYSTERIOUSLY MISSING. No – too literate. They wouldn't know how to spell "mysteriously", and it's got too many syllables for their readers. How about—'

'Oh, do stop it, Henry!' said Mrs Bagthorpe crossly. 'You take nothing seriously.'

'Except, of course, himself,' said Grandma.

Jack finally winkled Zero out of the woods and arrived back at the house.

'What's going on?' he asked. 'What are all these police doing here?'

'You may well ask,' his father told him. 'They came out to search for you. Why in the name of all that is wonderful can you not notify your family when you take to the hills?'

Jack's eyes went to the pepper mill.

'But I did,' he protested. 'I wrote it on an envelope and propped it on the table where you'd see it. I—'

'A *buff* envelope, Jack dear?' inquired his mother, darting a meaning look at her husband.

Jack, still scanning about, spotted the screwed-up envelope where Mr Bagthorpe had flung it earlier.

'There it is!' He picked it up and smoothed it out. 'See – gone camping—'

'It rather looks as if the police were called out on a fool's errand, Henry dear,' said Mrs Bagthorpe. 'You must hope that charges will not be brought for wasting police time.'

'Rats! That tramp's gone missing as well, hasn't he, and that unholy infant, *and* a couple of—'

'But Henry, that is merely cause and effect,' she told him, interrupting his bluster. 'None of this would have happened had not Jack been presumed missing in the first place.'

'That is true, madam,' said Handler Two, eager to find a scapegoat. 'Here, sonny, give me that note. It may be required as evidence.'

'You give it here!' said Mr Bagthorpe, forestalling him and snatching the note from Jack's grasp. 'That is *my* property.'

'Then it is a pity you did not read it, Henry,' said Grandma, delighted by this turn of events. With any luck, she reflected, her son could end up doing time. He was certainly obstructing the police in their inquiries.

'I must warn you, sir, not to destroy that item,' said Two.

Mr Bagthorpe, at bay, glared at the officers. He looked as if he were about to cram the incriminating envelope into his mouth and swallow it, in the best tradition of spy stories.

'Zero and me'll go out and see if we can track anyone down,' Jack offered, in a generous attempt to draw the fire off his father.

'Ha! That'll be the day!' snapped Mr Bagthorpe ungratefully. 'The day that pudding-footed, numb-nosed hound tracks anything down will be the day Mother wins the Nobel Peace Prize!'

Here again he was to be proved wrong – and in front of witnesses. Jack and Zero went out and it was they, later that night, who finally discovered the slumbering Daisy nestled against her wolves. The gratitude of the police knew no bounds. They kept calling Jack 'a bright lad', in between efforts to calm a near-hysterical Daisy Parker. From what anyone could gather she had set her heart on acquiring the police dogs as pets, and was frustrated to find that her father was not there to make an immediate offer for them.

'Where dat bad daddy!' she screamed. 'Where is he?'

'Cleared off,' said Mr Bagthorpe. 'True to form.'

'My daddy's rich as Crocus!' Daisy informed the bewildered police, who had not yet seriously taken on board the fact that she intended to adopt their fully trained animals and mix them in with Billy Goat Gruff and his four reputed grandfathers.

They made to go and put the dogs back in the van, but were prevented by Daisy. She locked her arms tightly about the neck of one Alsatian, and held on.

'Come!' commanded Handler One. The dog came, all right, but so did Daisy, her heels dragging on the floor.

'Let go!' commanded the handler. Daisy Parker, however, was not fully trained to obey commands. She merely tightened her stranglehold and started to scream again.

'Gramma Bag! Gramma Bag! Don't let them take my wolfs!'

Her grandmother was delighted that Daisy should thus appeal to herself.

'I must say, gentlemen,' she told the police, 'that I never expected to see an innocent child man-handled in this way. Especially in front of witnesses,' she added.

'Are those animals trained to kill?' asked Mr Bagthorpe. 'Because if so, now's the time to test 'em out.'

'The child is perfectly safe,' said Handler Two. 'She has only to loosen her hold and we can proceed.'

'I not let go, I not! I never let go for never and ever!'

This announcement, given Daisy's obsessive nature, sounded like deadlock.

Rosie had an inspiration.

'Ask them to swap for your Grandpa Gruffs, Daisy,' she said. 'You've already got two of them at home.'

'Awight, awight, I'll swap!' squealed Daisy.

The policemen were baffled. It was some time before they understood the transaction being offered, and when they did they turned it down flat. They again tried to leave, but Daisy still hung, a dead weight, on the dog's neck.

'Get my daddy, get my daddy!'

'Good idea!' said Mr Bagthorpe.

By now Uncle Parker would be back at The Knoll in bed and asleep. Mr Bagthorpe liked the idea of waking him up and fetching him back. It occurred to him that Uncle Parker might even be had up for attempting to bribe the police. He accordingly went into the hall and dialled the Parkers' number. His annoyance when he discovered that an answering machine had been installed was extreme. He heard three rings, and then Uncle Parker's cheerful voice:

'Hallo there, whoever you are. Russell Parker here, spouse of Celia and pa of Daisy. We're none of us in the mood for answering the phone right now. You can always try ringing again – we do sometimes turn this thing off. Or you can leave a message after the music. Cheers!'

The music was 'The Dead March' from Saul. Mr Bagthorpe was so thrown that he slammed down the receiver. His antipathy to answering machines was well-known, and probably Uncle Parker's main reason for installing one. After a few minutes collecting himself and working out a few pithy off-the-cuff insults, Mr Bagthorpe redialled the number and delivered his (more or less unprintable) message. He then stamped back into the kitchen.

'He's got one of those all-fired answering machines. You'll have to get over there,' he told the police. He looked ill-temperedly about him and his eye fell on the gently snoring Mrs Fosdyke.

'Ye gods!' he exclaimed. 'I shall kill her!'

He strode over as if he had every intention of doing this, even though watched by six policemen. In the event, however, he merely thrust his head forward and yelled, 'Boo!'

The effect was electric. Mrs Fosdyke's whole person convulsed, her head flew back, her arms went up and she and the chair went over with an almighty crash. Mrs Fosdyke let out an ear-splitting screech. This was evidently on a frequency that blew the police dogs' skulls, because they both jerked violently forward and Daisy was dislodged.

'Quick!' yelled Handler One. 'Now!'

The handlers and their dogs made smartly off. Daisy picked herself up and was after them in a flash, but they were too quick for her. They slammed the front door behind them. Daisy tried in vain to reach the latch, but it was too high for her, so she resorted to kicking it and banging it with her fists, screaming non-stop.

What with that and Mrs Fosdyke sprawled screeching on the floor in the kitchen, where Mr Bagthorpe was doing a lot of yelling, bedlam was now let loose.

If the cracked Valkyries had been on they would have been up against stiff competition.

It was ages before the household finally went to bed and settled. Daisy was lured up to Rosie's room by taking the two spare Grandpa Gruffs with her and being given the promise that in the morning negotiations for the police wolves would be reopened. Mrs Bagthorpe, who did not feel like driving yet again to Coldharbour Road, coaxed Mrs Fosdyke into staying over-night.

'Then you can have a good long lie in,' she promised. 'And I will bring you up a nice cup of tea.'

Luckily Mrs Fosdyke did not realize that Mr Bagthorpe had yelled in her ear, thus causing her to topple over. She thought that she had had a sudden nervous attack, and was quite frightened.

'Shall I go mad? Shall I go mad?' she kept asking.

'Of course not, dear,' Mrs Bagthorpe told her soothingly. 'Just go back to sleep. Sleep is a great restorer.'

Mrs Fosdyke made her employer place spare pillows on the floor by the bed, in case she should have another nervous seizure in the night. She was so confused that she would have gone to bed still wearing her hat, had not Mrs Bagthorpe removed it.

Mrs Fosdyke lay gazing owlishly up for a moment.

'I shall say my prayers,' she finally said.

Her eyes closed and Mrs Bagthorpe thankfully put out the light. She then went to check on her seriously ill elder son. She found him asleep, still wearing his head-phones. He had resorted to these to drown out the noise from below. No Bagthorpe could ever bear to be left out of any action, and it was particularly galling to William to know that his own shamming illness had cut him off from a first-class shouting match.

'Dear boy,' murmured his mother fondly.

One by one the lights of Unicorn House went off. Mrs Bagthorpe, before falling asleep, had a few last Positive Thoughts.

'I am sure Mr O'Toole will have found a safe haven,' she thought. 'And tomorrow – or rather today – is another day.'

She slept then, for some five or six hours. On waking she lay and had a few Positive Thoughts about the day ahead. (She always did this, despite the lack of evidence that it did any good whatsoever.)

'Today will mark a new step forward,' she told herself. 'Today we shall start the move towards liberation!'

She performed her yoga and Breathing exercises and went down. There she cleared and washed up the coffee cups from the previous night. She then went into the pantry and there tripped headlong over the bucket of goldfish, by now well and truly pickled in brandy.

'What a mercy that I discovered them before Mrs F.,' she thought Positively, as she picked herself up. She eyed the goldfish with repugnance and pondered how best to get rid of them.

'I could flush them down the lavatory,' she thought, 'but perhaps that would not be wise. I could empty the bucket in the garden, but that could be unhygienic and perhaps endanger plant life. I cannot empty gallons of water into the dustbin.'

In the end she fetched a fish slice, lifted the occupants of the bucket out one by one and dropped them in the waste bin. She averted her eyes and shuddered as she performed this nauseous task. The smell was horrible. The goldfish disposed of, Mrs Bagthorpe gamely picked up the bucket and sloshed its contents down the sink. She screamed. She had overlooked one of the dead fish, and it now lay, bloated and mottled on the stainless steel, looking like a still-life of the Surrealist school.

Mrs Bagthorpe wielded the fish slice again and then gave it a thorough scalding.

'Though I expect the alcohol acted as an antiseptic,' she told herself.

After this some people might have gone straight back to bed and stayed there. Mrs Bagthorpe, however, was made of sterner stuff (as, indeed, she needed to be). She turned on Radio Four in an effort to achieve some kind of hold on reality, and posted up on the noticeboard her House Rules and Rota of Duties.

She then prepared a tea tray and took it up to Mrs Fosdyke, who was just waking.

'Good morning, Gladys,' cried Mrs Bagthorpe gaily. 'I hope you slept well?'

'I 'ad some 'orrible dreams,' Mrs Fosdyke told her. 'Full of policemen they was and buckets of dead fish and that Daisy Parker.'

Mrs Bagthorpe wisely refrained from telling her that these had not been dreams, but stark reality. She helped prop Mrs Fosdyke up on her pillows and poured her tea.

'Nice nightie, this,' remarked that lady, fingering the lace trimmed satin of the garment lent to her. It was certainly a far cry from her own line in night attire.

'It is, rather,' agreed Mrs Bagthorpe. Encouraged by this she perched girlishly on the edge of the bed and prepared for a tête-à-tête.

'This is going to be a rather special day in our calendar, Mrs Fosdyke dear,' she confided.

'Why? What date is it?' she inquired suspiciously.

'It will mark a new beginning,' Mrs Bagthorpe went on. 'For myself, for you and for the girls.'

'Why?' demanded Mrs Fosdyke again.

Mrs Bagthorpe then outlined her plans for an equal division of household chores between the sexes. Her listener was not easily converted.

'It's not that Women's Lib you mean, I 'ope,' she said. 'I don't 'old with it. And I ain't wearing trousers, neither.'

'Oh, I shan't expect you to,' Mrs Bagthorpe assured her. 'But you must surely have noticed that the male members of this household do not pull their weight.'

''*E* don't,' said Mrs Fosdyke, meaning Mr Bagthorpe.

'Precisely. And that is what has to change.'

''E never will,' said Mrs Fosdyke with conviction. 'Tortoises don't change their spots. Nor leopards their stripes.'

'It will be difficult, certainly,' agreed Mrs Bagthorpe. 'But today we shall make a start. You, for instance, will do nothing at all but prepare meals.'

'Occasional Thurpy,' put in Mrs Fosdyke. 'Like my knitting.'

'When you are not cooking, you shall knit,' affirmed Mrs Bagthorpe. 'Today's Rota has Henry down for the hoovering. And Jack—'

'Not *my* 'oover,' interposed Mrs Fosdyke swiftly. 'I'm not 'aving that broke by him.'

'Oh, there is no danger of that,' said Mrs Bagthorpe, with more conviction than she in fact felt.

'I think 'e ought to go out and buy 'is own,' said Mrs Fosdyke obstinately. 'When I'm feeling meself, I fair enjoy a good 'oover.'

This was true. In the normal run of things Mrs Fosdyke rambled about the house pushing her sweeper with every sign of enjoyment. She had a technique all her own, which involved banging the machine regularly against skirting boards, particularly in the vicinity of the study, and sucking up the fringes of oriental rugs. Mr Bagthorpe said that he could bang in an insurance claim every time she hoovered.

'Except that they'd never believe it,' he said.

''E'll 'ave to get 'is own,' repeated Mrs Fosdyke.

'Oh dear!' Then Mrs Bagthorpe's face slowly brightened as an idea took shape. 'It is his birthday next week!'

15

Meanwhile at The Knoll, Uncle Parker had jogged
two miles and was just making coffee when the
buzzer sounded to indicate visitors. He picked up
the intercom.

'Hallo there! That you, Laura?'

'Police, sir.'

He hesitated. He could refuse to let them in. On
the other hand, he was harbouring a missing person
and had no real wish either to keep that person, or
to end up in jail himself. Besides, he felt quite frisky,
and usually rather enjoyed baiting the police.

'Good morning, gentlemen,' he greeted them.
'Come in, why don't you?'

He pressed the switch to operate the gates and
waited. The police car drew up at the front door
with its blue light flashing. That, Uncle Parker rightly
guessed, was a ploy to intimidate him and even up the
score. Policemen do not like being kept waiting by
electronic gates for permission to enter.

Uncle Parker waited a full two minutes before
answering the repeated chiming of the front door.

'Oh, there you are, gentlemen!' he exclaimed as he

opened the door and recognized two of the police-men from the previous night. 'Slept well, I trust?'

The police, who had not slept at all, and knew that Uncle Parker knew this, were frosty in their response.

'You will no doubt be pleased to hear that we have recovered your daughter, sir,' said One, his tone implying that fathers who take themselves off to bed while their four-year-old daughters are missing should be put on a charge.

'Oh, I knew she'd turn up!' Uncle Parker told them blithely. He had not the foggiest idea what they were talking about, having departed before Daisy went missing. 'Daisy always comes up trumps!'

'She was harbouring our missing animals,' said Two accusingly.

'I don't doubt it,' said Uncle Parker. 'Great animal-lover. All creatures great and small, and all that.'

'There is still, however, the matter of the missing millionaire outstanding,' said One.

'The what?'

'A Mr O'Toole, we understand,' said Two.

'Good grief!' exclaimed Uncle Parker. 'You are, of course, joking.'

'This is not a joking matter, sir,' said One lugubriously.

'If you had seen O'Toole when he first surfaced,' said Uncle Parker, 'or indeed smelled him, I do not fancy you would be bracketing him with Paul Getty. Who says he's a millionaire?'

'The information was given by Mrs Bagthorpe

senior,' replied Two. 'He is an old friend of her husband's.'

'Ah, I see.' Light was indeed beginning to dawn.

Uncle Parker could not even begin to guess Grandma's motives in vouchsafing this untruth, but he well knew that if she saw the chance to spin a web of intrigue and deception, embracing all possible, she did so. Grandma, as Mr Bagthorpe often said, left Lucrezia Borgia standing (though she had not yet, so far as was known, poisoned anybody).

Uncle Parker calculated his next move. He was forestalled, however, by the simultaneous appearance in the hall behind him of his wife and the missing millionaire.

A complicated scene then ensued. It appeared that Mr O'Toole, having woken to find himself in a strange hostel, had started to ramble about exploring the facilities. In so doing he had rambled straight into the Bower. Aunt Celia had not turned a hair. She recognized him at once, and saw it as the most natural thing in the world that one who was intended as her personal guru should materialize in her room. That sort of thing, after all, was always happening in fairy tales, and Aunt Celia certainly believed in *them*.

Mr O'Toole stood swaying slightly in his now crumpled frock while Aunt Celia in her lace and satin négligé clung to his arm and gazed adoringly up at him. The scene put one in mind of the transmogrified Bottom and Titania.

'He shall stay for ever,' she cooed. The police were

open-mouthed. Even Uncle Parker was momentarily nonplussed.

'I take it you are staying here voluntarily and of your own free will, sir,' Officer One asked Mr O'Toole unnecessarily.

He was warmly assured that this was the case.

'One last question,' said Two, who saw a faint chance of getting Grandma on a charge. 'Are you – er – are you a millionaire?'

'Of course I am!' cried Mr O'Toole, who had not the least notion why he had been asked this. 'The world is my oyster! I am more than a millionaire – I am a king!'

'Thank you. Thank you, sir,' Two stammered. He began to back away. 'We're sorry to have troubled you.'

He did not add 'Your Highness', but you could see that it was on the tip of his tongue. The police drove off, leaving Uncle Parker to finish his breakfast and Aunt Celia to consult her new guru.

Back at Unicorn House, of course, that gentleman was still presumed missing. His absence was felt most keenly by Grandma, Grandpa and Mrs Fosdyke. The latter had an illformed and treacherous plan to track down the missing millionaire herself, and offer him her services.

Mr Bagthorpe and his elder son were still in bed. The former said he would probably stop there for a week. The latter faintly said that he was feeling a little better, could probably manage a light breakfast of ham and eggs, and would move into the summerhouse for a few days' convalescence.

His siblings, when told this, were furious. None of them believed in William's illness (and Jack, of course, knew it to be a sham, though loyally did not say so). Mrs Bagthorpe's House Rules and Rota had been scrutinized and pronounced unfunny and unfair. Given that Mr Bagthorpe and William were in bed, all that day's chores and possibly those for the foreseeable future would have to be divided between the three of them.

'It's Mother's fault,' said Rosie bitterly. 'If she hadn't chucked that brick through Fozzy's window, *she* would have done everything.'

'Mother should do the housework herself,' Tess agreed. 'She could deal with those Problems in no time at all if she organized herself properly.'

Feelings of sisterhood were already fraying at the edges. There was certainly little sense of liberation. After breakfast, instead of scooting and banging about the house as usual, Mrs Fosdyke announced her intention of going for a walk.

The younger Bagthorpes stared. Such a thing had never before been known.

'Just a little stroll,' she explained guiltily. She was really, of course, going to look for Mr O'Toole. Mrs Fosdyke never strolled. She scuttled from A to B, head down and legs working like pistons.

They watched her go. A silence fell on the house.

'Where's Daisy?' Rosie asked.

No one knew. She had last been seen towing her Grandpa Gruffs off by their antlers.

'Let's beat it while Mother's not here,' said Rosie. 'Come on – outside. We'll play the Name Game. Got the list, Jack?'

He nodded. All three of them hurried in Mrs Fosdyke's wake into the garden. She had already strolled out of sight. The trio made for the potting shed and Jack produced the list.

The Name Game referred to was in fact a list of suggested names for Aunt Celia's forthcoming lickle stranger.

'Read it out, Jack,' Tess told him. 'Girls first.'

'Lucrezia. Cassandra. Pandora. Medusa. Why do they all end in "a"?'

'Sharon!' said Rosie, and giggled. 'The boys are better. Read the boys.'

'Atilla. Bede. Coriolanus. Adolph. Wogan. Mephistopheles. Cliff. Pius. Shylock. Sherlock. Methuselah. Wayne. Socrates. Othello. That's it.'

'Duke!'

'Dolly!'

'Goneril!'

'Anonymous!' Jack was well pleased with his suggestion and the others tittered gratifyingly. It almost made him feel equal.

'Ayatollah! Can you see it at play school? "Now, Ayatollah dear, I want you to draw me a nice pussy cat!"'

'Now that's very naughty, Shylock!'

'Put that box *down*, Pandora. Pandora, did you hear me? *Now* look what you've done!'

'What if it's twins?'

'Goneril and Wayne!'

Soon they were rolling around helplessly. They extended their list, and went on, with typical Bagthorpian overkill, to triplets, then quads.

Back at the house, Mrs Bagthorpe took William a lightly boiled egg, toast and tea, and ignored bawled requests from her husband for similar service.

'You are not ill!' she called back. 'Get up and get your own!'

'I would welcome a cup of tea myself, Laura,' came a voice from Grandma's room.

'I'm too busy.'

'Where is darling Daisy? She could bring it to me.'

'I don't know! I don't care!' Mrs Bagthorpe knew that this sounded Negative, but did not care.

'What?' came an enraged cry. 'You mean to say that—'

Mr Bagthorpe was out of bed in a flash and down the stairs to check his study. His wife hurried after him.

'While you are down there, check the Rota in the kitchen,' she told him. 'You are down for hoovering.'

He rattled furiously at the study door and found it locked. He gasped with relief, though he did not remember having locked it, nor where he had put the key. (This was not surprising. After an early-morning visit Daisy Parker had herself locked the study door behind her and pocketed the key.)

Mr Bagthorpe stomped into the kitchen and banged around getting himself breakfast. He banged as loudly as ever Mrs Fosdyke had done.

'When I've had this I shall get over to Russell's place,' he announced. 'I shall take a mallet and smash his front gates, and then I shall smash his answering machine.'

One of Mr Bagthorpe's chief pleasures in life was conducting monumental rows with his brother-in-law over the telephone. He could already feel withdrawl symptoms setting in.

'How very silly and childish,' his helpmeet told him. 'And how very typical. Russell outmanoeuvres you at every turn.'

Mr Bagthorpe was maddened by this undeniable truth.

'I should never have married,' he told her. 'I should've been like Wordsworth. Look how Dorothy ran around after him! She knew a true creative spirit when she saw one.'

'Wordsworth did marry, eventually,' she told him coldly. 'And I hardly see Celia playing Dorothy to your Wordsworth.'

Mr Bagthorpe was momentarily stumped. No one, however powerful his imagination, could see Aunt Celia tending bean rows, making broth and walking twenty miles in the rain to post a letter.

'Why do you always have to take everything I say literally?' he demanded. 'Can you not catch the spirit of the thing? It is the mark of a small mind to spell out ps and qs.'

'Then that is what I have,' she returned. 'And how very lucky for this household. Someone has to dot the ps and cross the qs.'

Just then, with her impeccable sense of timing, Grandma entered. She had a nose like a bloodhound for a brewing Row.

'Alfred is much put out by the loss of his friend,' she announced. 'Apparently he and Mr O'Toole had planned a fishing trip.'

'Surely he is not our responsibility?'

'I would not even use the word responsibility in the same sentence as that great stinking brute,' said Mr Bagthorpe. 'Are the police going after him for all that Scotch he downed?'

'I am surprised at your attitude, Laura,' Grandma told her daughter-in-law, ignoring her son. 'Mr O'Toole was a guest under your roof.'

'I know! I know! But what am I to do?' cried Mrs Bagthorpe, her own problems mounting by the minute. The likelihood of her finding time to answer any professional Problems seemed scant. She made another effort to put into practice her Plan for Liberation.

'Look Henry, look Mother,' she said in a tight, high voice. 'We are in a state of emergency.'

'We are always in a state of emergency,' put in Mr Bagthorpe.

'We must all pull together,' she went on, ignoring him. 'It is a case of all hands to the wheel.'

'For crying out loud, Laura,' said her husband, 'you sound exactly like some politician on a party political broadcast.'

'And a change in the running of this household is long overdue,' she continued. 'Women and girls are not mere skivvies. There must be an equal division of labour between the sexes!'

There followed a small silence.

'Finished?' inquired Mr Bagthorpe.

'I'm sure I don't have the faintest notion what you are talking about, Laura,' said Grandma. '*I* have never felt myself to be oppressed.'

Mrs Bagthorpe looked wildly about her.

'Oh, where are Rosie and Tess?' she cried desperately. 'Henry – read the Rota! Mother – read the Rota!'

Mr Bagthorpe, hands in pockets, sauntered over and cast his eye over the House Rules and the Rota. Grandma peered over his shoulder.

'I can make nothing of it,' she said. 'I have never been good at timetables.'

'See, Mother – here! I have put you down for flower arrangement today. All your duties are light!'

The idea of flower-arranging in fact quite appealed to Grandma. She could already see, in her mind's eye, bunches of stinging nettles and thistles in Ming vases, all kinds of hideous minglings of colours.

'Very well,' she agreed graciously. 'Darling Daisy shall assist me.'

'And you, Henry, are down for hoovering,' repeated

Mrs Bagthorpe, emboldened by Grandma's surprising acquiescence.

'So you keep telling me,' he replied. 'You know as well as I do, Laura, that my health is threatened by the vibrations of the thing.'

'Rubbish!' she snapped. 'That is merely an excuse, and you know it!'

'In any case,' he went on, 'there is something thoroughly unwholesome in this obsessive desire to track down every speck of dust. According to Quentin Crisp, if you leave dust for three months it never gets any worse. I suggest we test this theory.'

'Not according to Charles Dickens,' returned his wife. 'Have you never read *Great Expectations*?'

'I don't expect Miss Havisham's place was any worse than Quentin Crisp's,' replied Mr Bagthorpe. 'Dickens always went over the top with his descriptions.'

At this point Mrs Bagthorpe did something very strange. She screamed. She screamed on a long, high note.

The others stared. Mrs Bagthorpe, too, stared. She was as astonished as they. She had not felt the scream coming on. It had been quite without warning. Mrs Bagthorpe did not believe in screaming. She believed in Positive Thinking, Yoga, Breathing and Balance.

Mr Bagthorpe finally broke the silence.

'Have you gone mad, Laura?'

'I – I think I must have! Oh dear! Oh – oh—!'

She burst into tears and ran from the room.

'*Now* see what you have done, Henry,' said Grandma.

'Bilge. She's brought it on herself – all that crackpot stuff about rotas. She's got rotas on the brain!'

'Poor Laura,' remarked Grandma. 'Being married to you must be a sore trial. I think I will take my tea up to my room and write some Christmas cards.'

'You do that,' he told her.

Grandma always wrote her Christmas cards early, and often posted them in September. This was because she never seemed to receive as many as she sent out, and she hoped that early posting would remedy this. It never would. Many of her friends had over the years passed over where not even the last post would reach them. Her address book was hopelessly out of date.

Mrs Fosdyke came back from her stroll without Mr O'Toole. She started to prepare the lunch in the hope that he would turn up. No one had had time to shop, so she drew heavily on the contents of the restocked deep freeze.

The younger Bagthorpes, tired of their Name Game in the potting shed, returned warily to the house. They met William carrying a pile of rugs and pillows.

'Where d'you think you're skiving off to?' demanded Tess.

'I am putting myself in voluntary quarantine, in the public interest,' he replied. He dropped his bundle in order to open the summerhouse door.

'Me – me – Daisy Parker!' came a familiar squeaky voice.

William groaned. The others rushed to witness the inevitable Row, if not killing.

Daisy Parker, cheeks glowing, was in very heaven. She had visited the summerhouse only with the intention of taking up temporary residence with her Grandpa Gruffs (whose horns were now lavishly festooned with lavatory paper). Once installed she had inevitably started twiddling around with William's radio equipment. Her delight when she finally raised voices was boundless.

'Dat's der policemans, dat's der policemans, in't it? I know it is!' she burbled to her no doubt mystified contact. 'I got Billy Goat Gruff and I got Granpa Gruffs and wolfs and Arry Awk and now I got *you*!'

None of her conversations were very long, because she could not resist twiddling everything, and kept hopping from one contact to another.

William, confronted with this sight, let out a bellow of rage.

'Who dat? *Who* dat?' went on the imperturbable Daisy. 'Nonny who? Nonny Mus?'

'She's raised him!' Jack exclaimed. 'She's raised Anonymous of Grimsby!'

This lugubrious prophet of the airwaves had been unaccountably silent since the Bagthorpes' return from Wales. William had begun to despair of ever re-establishing contact. Now, Daisy had done it.

He could not rush forward and strangle her, as

he would have dearly liked to do, for fear that she would pull a switch or touch a dial. Anonymous from Grimsby's presence hung on a hair's breadth. William tiptoed forward.

'Oh – *Gimsby*!' said Daisy. 'What? No. I in't from Outer Space. Least, I *sink* I'm not from Outer Space. Daisy Parker, Daisy Parker calling!'

She was getting the hang of things quite well.

In the ensuing hush there drifted over from the house first the sound of the Hoover, and then a horrible cacophony which suggested that it had just sucked up a sock. (It had.)

'Dis is Daisy Parker an' I jus' decided I is from Outer Space. Gimsby, Gimsby, calling Gimsby – where are you, Nonny?'

Then, from the house, high-pitched screaming, on and on, screaming of an order never before heard, even by the Bagthorpes.

They looked at one another, awestruck.

'The Primal Scream!' said Tess at last in hushed tones. 'The Primal Scream!'

Mrs Bagthorpe was finally off her trolley.

THE BAGTHORPE SAGA

All Hodder Children's books are available at your local bookshop or newsagent, or can be ordered direct from the publisher. Just tick the titles you want and fill in the form below. Prices and availability subject to change without notice.

Please enclose a cheque or postal order made payable to *Bookpoint Ltd*, and send to: Hodder Children's Books, 39 Milton Park, Abingdon, OXON, OX14 4TD, UK. Email Address: orders@bookpoint.co.uk

If you would prefer to pay by credit card, our call centre team would be delighted to take your order by telephone. Our direct line *01235 400414* (lines open 9.00 am-6.00 pm Monday to Saturday, 24 hour message answering service). Alternatively you can send a fax on *01235 400434*.

TITLE		FIRST NAME		SURNAME	

ADDRESS	
DAYTIME TEL:		POST CODE	

If you would prefer to pay by credit card, please complete:
Please debit my Visa/Access/Diner's Card/American Express (delete as applicable) card no:

Signature...

Expiry Date...

If you would NOT like to receive further information on our products please tick the box. ❏